The Climb

By
Charlotte Blackwell

Contents

Chapter 1 2
Chapter 2 7
Chapter 3 10
Chapter 4 14
Chapter 5 17
Chapter 6 21
Chapter 7 25
Chapter 8 29
Chapter 9 34
Chapter 10 38
Chapter 11 43
Chapter 12 49
Chapter 13 53
Chapter 14 56
Chapter 15 60
Chapter 16 63
Chapter 17 66
Chapter 18 68
Chapter 19 72
Chapter 20 74
Chapter 21 77
Chapter 22 79
Chapter 23 82
Chapter 24 85
Chapter 27 88
Chapter 28 91
Chapter 29 95
Chapter 30 98
Chapter 31 100
Chapter 32 104

Chapter 33 107
Chapter 34 110
Chapter 35 114
Chapter 36 117
Chapter 37 120
Chapter 38 123
Chapter 39 126
Chapter 38 130
Chapter 39 134
Chapter 40 138
Chapter 41 141
Chapter 42 144
Chapter 43 147
Chapter 44 150
Chapter 45 153
The End 154

The Climb Copyright © 2018 by Charlotte Blackwell. All Rights Reserved.

All rights reserved. No part of this book may be reproduced in any form or by any electronic or mechanical means including information storage and retrieval systems, without permission in writing from the author. The only exception is by a reviewer, who may quote short excerpts in a review.

Cover designed by CJ Strange
Editing by Jodi Shaw

This book is a work of fiction. Names, characters, places, and incidents either are products of the author's imagination or are used fictitiously. Any resemblance to actual persons, living or dead, events, or locales is entirely coincidental.

Charlotte Blackwell
Visit my blog at www.charlotteblackwell.blogspot.com

Printed in the United States of America

First Printing: October 2018
JSLB Publishing

ISBN- 978-1-9993924-9-9

I want to dedicate this book to my husband James. He has shown me what true love is. I don't need to be a princess because he treats me like one every day. Thank you for all your support and love. I can't imagine life without you by my side.
xoxo

By, Charlotte Blackwell

Chapter 1

Trista

As we near the peak, each and every step becomes more difficult. We're only a few hours from the top of Africa's highest mountain. Soon the group I'm traveling with will reach the summit on Mount Kilimanjaro. I feel as if I weigh a ton; the oxygen at this altitude is thin. All the books I've read said the oxygen here is less than half of what it is at sea level. Every breath is a job all its own, almost as if no air is even reaching my lungs. I can see the air escaping my lungs as I breathe out into the cool air. The sight of it reassures me that I'm getting the oxygen I need. It's harder than I thought, but this is worth every struggle and I wouldn't change it for anything.

I've never seen such beauty before. The stars are amazing; thousands of shining balls of gas have never looked more beautiful. I feel as if I could just reach out and touch them. The horizon reaches as far as the eye can see, lit only by the blue moon and stars above. We're higher than the cloud cover, so it looks like a fine mist reaching for us from the ground below. The air is crisp and clean, like fresh laundry. The snow on the ground sparkles like thousands of diamonds from the reflection of the moonlight. With each step we take, you can hear the crunch of the snow beneath our feet. Thankfully, there isn't a lot; I couldn't imagine doing this in snow that was knee-deep. This, the final day of our ascent, is done at night. I can't wait to sit at nearly 6000 meters above sea level to watch the sunrise. The last five days have been just what I needed.

If you had asked me even a year ago if I thought I would ever go to Africa, I would've laughed. I never thought joy like this was possible for me. I have a great family, a tolerable job, and a few amazing friends; I thought that was all I needed. The past decade or so, I haven't really allowed people to get close to me. Not after him... after Jack. He destroyed all future relationships for me. I never thought one person could have such an impact on one's life, but he did. He destroyed the strong, confident woman I once was. I decided to take this trip for me; I guess you could call it a self-discovery trip. I'm tired of being the victim of a man that is no longer a part of my life, and conquering this mountain is exactly how I'm going to let his terrible words and actions go. Today I'm taking back my life and allowing others back in.

    There are ten people in our group, unfamiliar to each other...but we all came here, called by the adventure that not one of us could ignore. We began our adventure as strangers, but now we trek up the mountain as friends. When you spend five entire days with nothing to do but get to know each other, bonds can form quickly. In the past five days, we've learned so much about one another. We've shared stories, emotions, and feelings that normally take months. We have forged lifelong friendships, everyone watching out for one another, as each step gets more difficult. Our concern for each other is genuine; we want each member of our group to succeed on the most difficult leg of our trek. I've never felt safer, or carried more confidence in myself or the people that I'm surrounded by. I feel that I'm finding myself again. This is not for the faint of heart; climbing Kili is difficult on the mind, soul, and body. It's common for people to have to turn back, for either injury or altitude sickness - something that affects many climbers.

    The hike has taken us through various climates. From desert-like conditions where the ground is dry, and a few small, bush-like trees are scattered, to a beautiful forest setting with lush indigenous vegetation. Now we're surrounded by snow and damper ground. The snow's twinkling on the tree branches, as if they are draped in jewels. I'm amazed at the ecosystem here... nature in its full beauty. As we all admire our surroundings - the trees, the skyline, even the ground beneath our feet - I hear a deep beautiful voice. "How are you doing Trista?"

    "Not bad... a little woozy. What about you, Phil?" It feels like twenty minutes just to get one sentence out as I huff from the thin atmosphere.

    "Good. Starting to get a headache though."

    "Altitude sickness?"

    "Yeah, I think so. Thank God, we're almost there," he admits.

    "I'm right behind you if you need anything. Did you take any altitude pills?"

    "Yeah, I did. Thanks."

    I can't help but wish I had more guts. Phil is like the perfect man. He's the perfect height of six feet, with dirty blond, slightly wavy hair, and eyes as blue as the Caribbean, with tiny little laugh lines springing out from the corners. And handsome... oh yes, handsome. He has a good job as an investment banker and is so kind. He told me he holds a degree in English, but as he says, all he can do with that is ask 'Would you like fries with that?' So, he decided to do something more productive that can pay the bills. From what he tells me, investment banking was the perfect choice for him… a work-a-holic. We've been getting to know each other. He's opening up to me about his wife… she passed away a year ago. My heart aches for him; he speaks so highly of her, and obviously loved her dearly. When he talks about her, it's as if he drifts into his own little world. His eyes grow distant and the pain's visible - the sadness evident behind his smile. I want to reach out to him, to hold him and let him know he's not alone in this world. From what Phil tells me, climbing Kilimanjaro was one of his wife's dreams, but she died from cancer before she could fulfill it. So here he is on the anniversary of her death, making the climb for her.

Now drifting into my own little world, I start daydreaming about having a love like Phil's and stop focusing my attention on the hike. Each step gets more difficult as the trail becomes more snow covered. The rocks beneath the snow are loose and with each step, I find my concern growing. Without warning, the rocks slip from under me and I trip on the path. I let out a raspy yelp as I fall in agony.

"Trista, what happened? Are you okay?" Phil gasps, as he drops to my side.

Tears stream down my face, "My ankle. I twisted it or something; I tripped on a rock. I'm such a klutz," I cry out with embarrassment.

The entire group struggles in the high altitude to get to my side. Phil already has my leg on his, and is trying to remove my boot to inspect my injury. He tenderly unlaces it, careful not to cause further injury. Slightly pulling the tongue of the boot with the gentlest motion, he pulls it from my foot, revealing a small white ankle sock.

"Awe, beautiful, your ankle's already swollen. He pulls out a white tube sock from his knapsack and fills it with sparkling snow from the side of the mountain. "Here, this may help the swelling to slow down. I don't know if you'll be able to continue, though. I'm so sorry."

The tour leader comes to inspect my ankle for himself. "Phil's right, Trista, you can't walk on that. We need to get you back down the mountain." The tall lanky African man with his tight afro tries to comfort me with a smile.

If the people native to this area can climb this mountain with nothing more than old tire pieces strapped to their feet, I can do this too. One thing that we receive when committing to such a trek like Kilimanjaro is porters; local residents that assist the climbers in carrying up sleeping quarters such as tents and sleeping bags. They also carry a mobile kitchen of sorts. We're provided with a chef that cooks all our meals to ensure we're properly nourished for such a hike. Our porters do this every day at lightning-fast speeds. They find anything they can to strap to their feet and don't complain, so I'm sure I can do this. "Are you freakin' kidding me? We are only a few hours from summit. I can make it," I cry out, not even realizing Phil called me beautiful.

The Climb

"Trista, we're going to have to carry you back down this mountain. Between the altitude and that swelling, something serious could happen," Afram insists, in his heavy African accent.

I notice Phil take Afram off to the side; I can faintly hear them in the background.

"Afram, we're so close to summit. If we must carry her down, why can't we carry her up? This way our entire team can finish together. We can take the fastest route down and ensure she's safe."

"Phil, I understand you want to finish as a group, but I just don't think it's safe."

"Then I'll stay with her."

As I hear Phil, I scream out, "Like hell, you will!"

The beautiful man wrapped tightly in his winter gear, walks back and kneels next to me. "I won't let you be the only one not to reach summit."

"And I won't let you give up because of me. You have meaning behind this; you want to put your wife's picture and that small vial of ashes on the summit. You have to finish for her, finish for Sara."

Phil becomes somber and takes a breath, "Trista, you are an amazing woman, thinking about me and my wife's picture when your dream is ending right now. I refuse to let this happen. We'll carry you up," he insists with authority.

Afram's reluctant, but nods and they prepare a makeshift cot from our tenting gear to carry me in. The team uses skills we all learned in our outdoor survival class. Using the tent poles and binding them together with rope and a tarp, they construct a fully functional cot.

It doesn't take long before we're on the move again. This trip has taught me so much about others and myself. I came to get away; I needed a change from my boring job and pathetic life. I am thirty-four years old and have nothing to show for it. I have no husband... not even a boyfriend, for that matter, and no children. All I wanted from this climb was to find myself, get out of my apartment, and see the world. Not only am I seeing the world, I'm seeing humanity at its finest. What a remarkable man Phil is; I'm so grateful for him and all the wonderful friends I'm making on this trip. This is the toughest part of the climb, partly due to the altitude and partly to the snow, and still, they're willing to haul my ass up the mountain. Where else could I ever find such a group of selfless humans altogether?

It takes almost twice as long as planned to summit. I only weigh 120 pounds, but at this altitude, I am sure it feels more like 500 to those carrying me. This is the most amazing sight I've ever seen in my life. The sun's just rising, and the skyline is painted a bright orange; it looks like the rays are reaching up from the ground to meet us. The white, snowcapped mountain makes it glow so much brighter, and the wooded summit sign is the perfect touch. We made it; we've found a small piece of heaven. I'm so blessed and grateful that my new friends helped me get here.

"How are you doing, Trista?" Phil asks as he helps me to sit up in the cot.

"I'm so happy right now I can't even feel the pain. Thank you for insisting on bringing me to the top. Now go get your picture taken as you place your wife's picture at the summit sign," I insist.

"I will, but first we need to get you up here for the group picture."

"Oh, please don't worry about me. I just feel so lucky to have this memory."

"Well, it won't be a group picture without the prettiest girl on the mountain." He smiles and then sweeps me up in his arms to carry me to the summit sign. The sign is simple; just a few brown boards nailed together with the site statistics painted in bright yellow, but for those of us that get to see it first hand, it's an accomplishment. Who would've known touching a silly piece of worn out wood could be so emotional, enlightening, and thrilling? As everyone gets their single pictures taken, I notice something change in Phil's demeanor; he takes the small vial of ashes and sprinkles them on top of the mountain under the sign. I can see he's emotional. He wipes tears from his face and kisses Sara's picture. Turning and lifting the corners of his mouth, he offers me a small smile. There must be a sense of closure for him, even though this is evidently difficult for him.

We don't stay long at the summit, as my ankle is swelling even more. It's also turning a lovely shade of violet and blue. Afram's afraid that if we don't get down and equalize properly, I could lose my foot. I try not to panic, but the tears flow freely down my face. The others carry me as Phil walks next to the cot, holding my hand. Something about him gives me a sense of peace, comfort, and belonging I've never felt before.

"Trista, don't worry. We'll get you down and we will get you help. I'll stay with you, I promise. Everything's going to be fine."

"I... I... can't... I... don't want to lose my foot," I cry.

"Listen to me; if I have to put you on my back and carry you down myself, I will. You are not going to lose anything. We've just had one of the most amazing experiences in the world, so focus on that." Phil lifts my hand and gives it a small kiss.

Chapter 2

Phil

I can't believe I did it. I climbed Kili for you, Sara. I lost you a year ago and I'll never forget you. My heart has ached for you since the day you left; I never thought I'd feel normal again. This trip, this moment, right here, right now, I finally feel closure, a sense of peace. I know with every inch of my being that you're here with me. Sara, you brought me here. I feel so guilty, being here for you and having feelings for this woman I just met. I know before you passed, you told me to find happiness, to move on and not pine for you. I didn't think I would ever be able to move on, to find someone that could even bring half a smile to my face. Did you do this? Did you bring Trista to me? I'll always love you, baby. Thank you for loving me back.

I can't help but wonder if this is Sara's doing, as I hold another woman's hand and help her through a difficult time. She has the same hands as Sara; slim long fingers, neatly trimmed nails with a neutral polish. They're soft, even after being in the elements for the past week. She has small age lines on the tops of her hands, and dimples between her knuckles. She doesn't wear any rings but has a simple charm bracelet that dangles from her wrist. Maybe this is what makes it feel so comfortable like I belong. "How are you doing, Trista? Can I get you anything?" I ask, looking down at the beautiful woman before me. I wasn't sure if I'd ever be interested in another woman after losing Sara, yet here I am, having feelings and thoughts I haven't had in a long time.

"I'm a little scared, to be honest, Phil, but thank you for all your help," Trista admits.

"I really don't want you to worry; you're going to be fine," I encourage.

Our group continues down the mountain. We take the fastest route down and agree to trek on, to get Trista to a hospital. The poor girl can't lose her foot. I can tell how hard she is on herself, without reason. She really doesn't know how beautiful she is. I look down at her tear-filled green eyes and start to imagine what life could be like with her.

"So, where is it you live again?" I ask, trying to get her mind off her injury.

"California. You're out east, right?" she replies.

"Yeah, I'm in a suburb of New York. Have you ever been out east?"

"Not yet, but I hope to make it there one day. I've always wanted to see a Broadway show."

"Oh, you really should. It is an experience all its own," I encourage.

She flashes me a beautiful smile, which beams brighter than the sun and catches me off guard, nearly knocking me off my feet. Our group puts her cot down for a lunch break; as usual, the porters trekked ahead of us, so they already have lunch prepared. We eat quickly so we can continue on our way; the group agrees to complete the descent today. During lunch, I check Trista's ankle again. I can see the pain she's in just by me pulling her sock down a little.

"I'm so sorry, beautiful. I just want to see how your foot's doing." I check for a pedal pulse to ensure the blood's still flowing. "It looks like the swelling's stopped. We only have about four more hours to go and we'll get you to the hospital." I assert.

Tears start ballooning in her eyes, making the green look like perfect cut crystals. "Thank you for taking care of me. I'm sorry that I've ruined the trek for everyone."

Candace, one of the other women on the climb with us, leans down and hugs Trista. "Kiddo, you haven't ruined anything. We're all happy to help; it wouldn't have been the same if we just sent you down with a porter. We're all friends now, and this is what friends do."

The other members of our group cheer in agreement. I wish it was me hugging Trista. To hold that petite little body in my arms, comforting her and letting her feel safe with me. I was so lucky to have had Sara in my life, to love her and enjoy her for as long as I did. I never expected to feel like that again, yet I think I feel more for this woman than I could have ever expected to again. Is this what love at first sight is? I wonder. I can't help but imagine what it'd be like to hold her in my arms and have her luscious pink lips press up against mine. The passion and excitement, I can envision it so clearly. Brushing my hand against her rosy cheek and slowly moving it through her long brown hair. Kissing her, the warmth of her breath against me.

"Phil, are you okay? What's going on in that head of yours?" Trista asks with concern.

I smile, "Yeah, just daydreaming."

"Oh, I can imagine. This must've been a very emotional experience for you, and me being a klutz and getting hurt has taken away from it. I can't tell you how sorry I am. Please, take as much time as you need," she says, not knowing she's the only thought in my head right now.

"It's emotional, but not for the reasons you may think. Really, I'm okay. Let's get you down and checked out. Most of all, stop apologizing. I wish you'd see how amazing you are."

She smiles and blushes a little before waving away my compliment. I've gotta figure out this girl. What happened to make her think she's not important? It drives me nuts... maybe the only thing I don't like about her.

Before long, we're back at the start, the same place this journey began. The medics see Trista on the cot and race out of the office. Afram explains what happened and they load her into the truck take off for the hospital. Our group gathers our items and all the equipment from our trek. Anything we no longer need, we leave in a pile for the porters to keep. The journey begins to sink in, as we all relax with an ice-cold Coke. We Americans come to this foreign land, with our expensive hiking boots and coats, while these men are wearing torn-up tire rubber strapped to their feet. I pull my boots off and toss them in the pile as well. Whatever we don't need for the remainder of our vacation gets donated. It's better than any tip we could give them, of course. I leave some cash I had in my pocket and an extra pair of shoes as a little surprise for them.

"Can you believe we did it?" Rob shouts.

"Yeah, that was so amazing. I can't believe Trista got hurt. I hope she's going to be all right. I wish I could go check on her, but my plane leaves in two days. I need to get back to the hotel and pack," Barb announces.

Trista, I can't believe I forgot about her, even for a split second. I need to find her; I can't just leave. I made her a promise when we were on Kili, that I'd be with her. The medics return after transferring her to the hospital to gather her belongings, so they can return them to her.

"May I come with you, please? I'd like to make sure she's all right," I ask politely, unsure of what the privacy laws are in Africa.

The medics agree, so I say my goodbyes to the rest of the group and jump in the truck. I need to make sure she's okay. I need to see her again; I can't let this be the last I see of her. I take one last look up at the mountain and say a silent goodbye to Sara. *'Love you, baby.'*

By, Charlotte Blackwell

Chapter 3

Trista

"The doctor will be with you shortly, Miss Smith. He's just reviewing your x-rays," the nurse informs me.

"Thank you," I reply, before drinking the water she just brought me.

Then she exits the modest room only to leave me with my thoughts. The pain medication is finally kicking in, and I no longer feel the constant throb from my foot. I can't believe I made such a fool of myself in front of Phil. I shake my head, thinking *'if I could only see him again.'* Ha! Who am I kidding? I could never just blurt out to a man that I'm interested in him. Thirty-four years and I have never had a serious relationship. Yet I find myself thinking about him, and what could happen if I *did* have the courage to tell him how I feel. Even though I don't understand these feelings, I know they're real. Just thinking about him, my heart starts to race.

I really wish he would've come here with me, but I can't expect a man I only met a few days ago to drop his entire vacation for me. Besides, what makes me think I'd even have a chance with him? He's handsome, intelligent, kind, funny, and so much more. What could he possibly see in me? I lay my head back on the pillow and close my eyes. All I see is Phil, looking back at me with his piercing blue eyes, and lashes that every woman would kill for. His dark blond hair that reminds me of a sandy beach, falling in his face as he bends down to kiss me. As our lips touch, a burning sensation shoots through my body, filled with passion and excitement. I imagine holding Phil, kissing him, wanting to be with him forever. I shake the thoughts from my head, knowing that it's nothing more than a dream.

"Miss Smith, sorry to bother you, but you have a visitor," the nurse announces.

"Please, call me Trista, but who could be here to visit me? I don't know anyone in Tanzania."

A deep voice answers, "I see you forgot about me already." Phil smiles as he enters the room.

My heart skips a beat, and the sight of him literally takes my breath away. I always thought that was just an expression, but it rings true when I see him. "Phil, what on earth are you doing here? You should be enjoying the rest of your vacation," I say, unsure if I can hide my excitement with the smile beaming across my face.

He walks over and sits in the chair next to my bed. "Are you kidding me? I promised you I'd be here and make sure you are okay. So, here I am, right by your side."

"Thanks, Phil, I'm just waiting for the x-ray results now."

"Okay, well I'll stay and wait with you if that is all right."

"Of course, I enjoy your company."

"I gathered your belongings after the climb and brought them here for you," he says, lifting my bag.

"Thank you again. So, is the rest of the group going back to their hotels or are they celebrating at Kilimanjaro?"

"Everyone was pretty excited to go back to their hotels and shower. They feel really bad that they can't come see you, but most of them depart in a few days."

"Oh, I completely understand. I'm so grateful that everyone went through so much to help me after I got hurt."

As we continue to talk a little, the doctor comes in. "Miss Smith, I have the results of your tests."

"And how do things look?" I ask.

Phil reaches over and holds my hand, sending a burning sensation through my entire body. Who knew just a simple touch from someone could set off a reaction like this. I feel the blood race through me and stop in my cheeks; I take a deep breath, awaiting the doctor's diagnosis.

"Well, you have a small hairline fracture. We'll need to put a cast on, but you'll be fine. The excessive swelling was caused from the high altitude. It should go down in just a day or two. We will use a temporary cast until then and put you in a plaster cast before you leave. I've ordered regular pain medication for you; I want to ensure you're comfortable," the tall, African doctor explains, his thick accent sometimes hard to understand.

"So, how long will I be hospitalized for?"

"Only until the swelling goes down and we can get the plaster cast on. You should be out of here by the weekend." He smiles, "I can see you two lovebirds want to enjoy the rest of your trip."

"Oh but ... we, um...." I get all flustered and can't get the words out.

Phil smiles. "Thank you, Doctor," he says, without correcting him.

The doctor nods, "I'll have someone come in and put on your temporary cast shortly." He turns and leaves, his clean shoes making a squeak as he moves across the floor.

We both have a little laugh; my heart's nearly pounding through my chest right now. I can't believe that Phil allowed the doctor to think we were a couple.

"So, that is great news. You'll be out of here in a few days."

"Yeah, what a way to spend my vacation," I mumble.

"How long until you leave?" he asks.

"Well, my flight isn't booked for another ten days. I wanted to experience more of Africa. What about you?"

"Two weeks left. I had some great things planned."

"Had? What happened that you don't have the plans anymore?" I question.

"Nothing really, but I want to stay here with you. I made you a promise and I intend to keep it," he admits.

"I appreciate that, but I don't want to ruin your trip. You heard the doctor... I'm fine."

"I know, but Trista I have to admit something. I have not felt like this in a long time. I enjoy your company and look forward to every minute I get to learn more about you. I *want* to be here with you."

My heart begins to flutter, "Phil, I enjoy being with you as well. I want you here, but do you really want to spend your vacation sitting in a hospital?"

"If it means I get to be with you, then yes, I do." He smiles.

Phil sits on the edge of my bed and gently brushes a strand of hair from my face. The blood instantly rushes back to my cheeks. Feeling almost feverish, I inhale the sweet scent of his cologne. Slowly, he leans in towards me and our lips touch ever so softly. With his palm against my cheek, he wraps his fingers around the back of my head and slightly pulls me towards him. I'm sure he can feel my heart pounding against my chest as he presses his lips into mine.

The door to my room opens. "Miss Trista," the nurse calls out.

Phil and I are caught off guard, both wrapped up in the moment. He jumps up and darts across the room as if we are teenagers who just got caught by my mom.

"Yes?" I respond, with a little giggle.

"I just thought we should get you washed up before your cast goes on," the nurse announces.

I realize that I'm a mess; I still haven't cleaned up after the climb. "That'd be wonderful," I agree.

Phil steps closer to the bed. "Would you like me to go to your hotel and bring you an overnight bag?"

"That would be great, thank you again, Phil."

I dig through my hiking bag and give him my room key, then write out a quick list of items I'd like, along with where he can find them.

"I'm at the same hotel, so this is great. I'll clean up a little as well. I don't know how much longer my shower in a can will work," he laughs.

"Shower in a can?" I crinkle my brow with confusion.

"My axe body spray, shower in a can." He winks.

I start to laugh; he's hilarious. "You're such a goof. Please, take your time. I bet you could use a nap and a meal as well."

"Nope, I'm good. A shower and your bag, that's all I need. Should I take your hiking bag back to the hotel for you?"

"Sure. You're the best," I announce, as I grab my personal belongings from the bag.

As Phil's leaving, he turns and gives me a quick kiss on the head. "I'll be back shortly."

Sitting here by myself before the nurse comes back to help me clean up, I realize what just happened. Phil kissed me; my heart starts pounding just at the thought. I never imagined anything could feel that good. The memory of his soft lips against mine takes over and I have trouble catching my breath again. How can he do this to me? I can't wait to see him again, but fear that he'll regret our kiss. It must have been awkward for him, kissing someone other than his wife. Still able to feel the sensation of his lips against mine, I lift my hand to my mouth and outline my lips with my finger. I'm imagining the day our lips will touch again... at least I hope they will. Never have I had such perfect, full lips touch me before. They were soft and passionate; our kiss was like one out of a romance movie. I can only hope it will have the same happy ending.

By, Charlotte Blackwell

Chapter 4

Phil

Arriving at the hotel, I go to my room first for a shower and a clean change of clothes. I place Trista's bag on the desk in the front room and walk down the marble-floored hall and through the French doors that separate the sitting area from the bedroom. The king size bed in the center of the room is so inviting. The large, full pillows and pillow top mattress taunt me. I toss my own bag on the bed and go to the washroom. Turning on the shower, I allow it to heat to the perfect temperature as I brush my teeth and shave. Trying to keep Trista from my mind for only a few moments proves to be impossible. Hiding the excitement, I had when I saw her at the hospital was near impossible. Even now, with just the thought of her, I can't seem to get rid of it. I can't help but wonder if she's thinking about me too.

The hot water pours down over my body, as I imagine Trista right here with me. Remembering the kiss, we shared back at the hospital, her tender lips pressing and moving in sync with mine, the taste of mint gum on her tongue… it was more tantalizing than I'd imagined. Picturing her standing here with me, bare, with the water falling over our bodies, we begin to kiss as I run my hand over her slender yet shapely body, and I pull her in close to me. Tilting my head back in the water, I try to wash the thoughts from my mind, but it is too late. As I lather the soap, I feel the rush of excitement as my heart nearly beats through my chest. I lean against the cold shower wall and try to calm myself with the thought of Trista still vivid in my mind. A deep breath in, and I can feel the excitement rising, wishing she were really here with me.

Every scenario runs through my mind. I can picture throwing her against the wall and kissing her with complete and unbridled passion. Moving my hands down her shapely body, I lift her and she wraps her legs around my hips. Continuing to kiss her, I brush my tongue across her neck to her ivory-skinned shoulder. Memorizing every curve of her body and sharing a passion I never imagined existed, my excitement grows with the fantasy, and I realize I can't wait to see her again. I'm feeling as if I should be guilt-ridden because of Sara, but I'm not. Of course, I love and miss Sara, but I feel like it's time to allow happiness back into my life. Trista just feels right. I sense I need her in my life; I *know* I want her in my life. My heart still aches from the loss of Sara, but I know she wanted me to find someone new to have a family with, to have what we never got the chance to have.

Once dressed, I grab Trista's bag and head to her room. The note says room 403; taking the elevator down to the fourth floor, I insert the key card into the door. I grab the laundry bag from the closet and place the items from her hiking bag in, leaving it by the door for housekeeping to take. Following the details on her note, I pack some clothing and personal items for her. In the bathroom, I find her make-up bag and throw it into the carry-on bag. I don't think she needs it; over the past few days on the mountain, she never even wore lip gloss and was still the most beautiful women I've ever seen. It doesn't take long to get her requested items; she's very organized.

I can't wait to get back to the hospital and see her again. It's been less than a week since I met Trista, and yet I find myself wanting to spend every moment with her. I make a quick stop at a sidewalk florist and get her some roses. I wish I knew what kind of flowers she likes; roses just seem so generic. Climbing Kilimanjaro was a great experience, and meeting Trista was even better, yet I find myself wanting to experience so much more with her. Maybe once she's released from the hospital, we can do some sightseeing together. We have to make the most of the time we have together.

My stomach growls at me, as I've forgotten to eat since we got off Kili. Walking through the tourist area of Tanzania, I find a nice little restaurant and stop in for a bite to eat. They have nice meals here in Africa, but I'll never understand why they always hide an egg and other crap in the middle of the rice in every meal. It isn't that I don't like it; it's very good. I just don't understand it. There are so many people in this country that are hungry, and yet they hide major sources of protein in the tourist's food. We'd happily eat it and still pay the same price even without the hidden treasure. They could charge us appropriately and feed the nation. Their portions are far superior to those back home. I hate to think of all the waste. I only wish there was something I could do to help the nation that showed me that it's okay to live my life even though I lost my wife.

By, Charlotte Blackwell

∞ ∞ ∞

Walking back to the hospital, I begin to feel like a schoolboy going to see his first crush; the thrill I'm feeling at the thought of seeing those beautiful eyes and long brown hair again. As I walk the streets, several young kids begin to follow me, their hands out looking for treats. I remembered to toss a bag of candy in Trista's bag, so I stop and take it out, giving the children a few pieces each. The light in their eyes when I hand them the candy could light the night sky. These children grow up with nothing, and yet have so much life in them. I'll have to tell Trista all about them. It will make her happy.

Who would've thought I'd meet someone who could make me feel again, here in Africa. I came to Tanzania for Sara, to fulfill her dream. I never had any real interest in climbing a mountain before, but I'm so glad I did. Sara had been the focus of my life for so long. Trying to make her happy and comfortable after we learned of her fatal brain tumor was my main goal. I forgot how to take care of myself. Now Sara's given me the best gift... the gift to feel again... to love again. I would've never met Trista if it weren't for Sara. *'Thank you, my love,'* I think, looking up to the heavens. I loved Sara so much and I always will; it's just nice to know there's room in my heart for another. Before Sara passed, she made me promise not to dwell on her. She wanted me to find love again. She told me I deserved to be loved and that any woman would be lucky to have me. I just didn't think it was possible. I didn't think I had room in my heart. Nor did I think any woman would be accepting of the fact that I loved Sara so much, but Trista seems to understand. I don't know if she's the one I'll spend my life with, but I do know she's the one to help me move forward.

The more I think about Trista, the faster I want to get back to her. Who falls for a woman they met only days ago and on the other side of the world? I might be losing my mind. Either way, I want to get to know her better and see where this may go. We have about a week to see things through. Reaching the hospital doors, I fight with thoughts of insecurity, wondering if I should go in and kiss those beautifully pink lips again. Once I finally pull myself through the front doors with flowers in hand, I continue to think of the kiss we shared and where it could've led, had the nurse not come in. I wanted nothing more than to whisk her up in my arms and take her back to the hotel with me.

Chapter 5

Trista

Not knowing how long Phil will be gone, I try to hurry cleaning up. With my ankle fracture, I can't put any pressure on my leg, so I'll need the nurse to help me shower.

The young nurse comes back in. "Miss Trista, I have a shower chair you can sit on. The only problem is, we can't keep your leg elevated, so we have to hurry, to prevent more swelling."

"That sounds good to me." I smile, and then I realize she really will need to help me wash. I hate others seeing me naked. Even at the gym or pool, I always use the private change rooms, but it's been nearly a week since I've showered, and those wet wipes just aren't cutting it anymore. I'll have to wear a hospital gown until Phil returns with my clothing, but at least I won't smell.

The nurse runs the water to a nice lukewarm temperature, as I sit in the cold shower chair with only a towel covering me. The moment it's ready, she wheels me under the running water and hands me a small bar of soap. The nurse is great, turning away and allowing me to wash with some privacy, only turning back to help with my injured leg. The entire shower only takes about five minutes, even though I would've loved to just relax and enjoy the warmth pouring over me. She helps me dry off, and to dress in the dull cotton gown, before wheeling me back to my bed.

"I'll get the doctor to place your temporary cast now," she says, as she puts a large foam wedge under my foot to help keep it elevated.

I smile, feeling refreshed, "Thank you for your help."

Before long, the doctor returns. "Miss Smith, you look much better. How is your pain?"

"I feel wonderful after my shower, thank you. The pain isn't too bad. A little tender, but tolerable."

"Great, although if you do experience pain, make sure you inform us. I still want to keep an eye on it, and ensure circulation is maintained," he informs. "Where is your husband?"

I smile. My husband... something I never thought I would hear. Even though Phil and I aren't married, I can't help but wonder what it'd be like to be Mrs. Phil... I don't even know his last name. "He is just a friend, but he should be back soon."

"Oh, my mistake, I'm sorry for the assumption."

"No... no need to apologize. So, we are putting this cast on till the swelling goes down, right?"

"Yes, I think it may even be sooner than I expected. Your foot's looking much better than when you came in a few hours ago. Elevating and icing it, is working. We'll put this cast on for tonight and check it again tomorrow. We may be able to fit you with a plaster cast then. I'll be back in the morning to check on you, but the nurses are here if you need anything."

"Thank you, Doctor. I'm sure I'll be fine."

Shortly after the doctor leaves, Phil walks in with my bag in hand and the other hand behind his back. My heart nearly leaps from my chest at the sight of him. He walks in slowly, peeking to ensure the medical staff isn't here and smiles when he meets my gaze. He looks even more handsome than before. His hair is styled with a little spike - a faux-hawk, I guess - and he shaved, so I can see every angle of his face. His smile meets the corners of his eyes and his eyelashes can practically reach across the room. The dark blue jeans he's wearing fit him perfectly, showcasing his thick, muscular thighs and his...

"Hey, hot stuff. How are you feeling?" he asks, while walking closer.

I try to pull myself up on the bed a little more. "Much better. Did you get something to eat and relax a little?"

"It felt so great to take a shower and just clean up a bit. Then I went to get your things." He holds up my bag. "I also got you these." His other hand comes out from behind his back, holding the largest bouquet of roses, in all different colors.

"Oh Phil, you didn't have to. Thank you so much. They're beautiful," I gush.

"They only hold a fraction of your beauty; it's my mission to make you feel special." He smiles and kisses my head.

"I think that altitude messed with your brain. Me, beautiful? Can I have some of what you're on?" I chuckle to brush off my insecurities.

"Nah – it's a true story." He smiles.

As he leans down, I take in his scent and melt. I can't help myself, so I pull him towards me and kiss him. The flowers fall to the floor and he sits on the edge of the bed, arms wrapping around me. We pull each other closer; the passion of the kiss is something I've never experienced before. Phil runs his hand along my face, cupping my head in his hand, and slowly moves his other hand up my side, passing my waist and moving slowly until he reaches around my back and holds me tight. Pins and needles run over my entire body, and I let out a little gasp as he pulls back.

Phil looks down and whispers, "Sorry, am I hurting you?"

"No... don't be, I was pleasantly surprised." My face starts to burn with embarrassment.

Phil reaches to the ground and picks up the flowers he brought me. "I don't understand what you're doing to me, Trista. I feel so alive when I'm around you."

"I feel the same; you make me feel so wonderful. I can't help but wonder if fate brought us together on that mountain." Realizing how stupid I sound, I regret my words almost instantly.

He leans in and kisses my head again.

"So, the doctor says I may get out of here tomorrow if the swelling continues to go down," I blurt out, quickly changing the subject.

"That is great news." He smiles. "I noticed you have a regular single room at the hotel. I have a suite with a living area. If you'd like, you're welcome to stay with me. That way I'll be there to help you and what not," he offers nervously.

"Wow! Move in already?" I joke.

"Umm... uh... I... there's a spare bedroom. I didn't mean..."

I start to laugh. "Phil, I know what you mean, I'm just teasing you. Thank you for the offer."

"But?"

"But, I don't want you to waste your vacation waiting on me."

"Well, if you haven't noticed, I'm kinda into you. There's nothing more I'd want to do than be with you, vacation or no vacation."

Tears slowly well up in my eyes as I listen to him.

"Are you okay? Do you need your medication?" he asks with concern.

"No, I'm fine. That's just the sweetest thing anyone's ever said to me." I wipe a tear from my face, knowing that this won't last.

"So, will you stay in my suite? I'd really love it. We've already spent every night together since we met," he jokes.

"Sure, I will... but as soon as you get tired of doting on me, you have to promise to take me back to my room."

By, Charlotte Blackwell

I can't believe he wants to spend more time with me, that he wants me to stay with him. My nerves begin to shoot off inside. I wonder if he suspects, but he doesn't seem to notice. I brush it off, not caring, just excited that he wants to spend more time with me so that we can get to know one another better. I want to learn everything about him; I want to hear about his family, about his childhood, about Sara. What's even more shocking to me is that I want to share my stories with him. No one back home is going to believe this... I'm not even sure if I believe it.

Chapter 6

Phil

I trace back and forth from Trista's hotel room to mine, moving her things. The doctors should be releasing her sometime today. I want to ensure everything's here, so she doesn't have to worry, and so she's comfortable. I've requested the hotel to fill the room with flowers from the area, as well as a traditional African dinner prepared and ready for our return. She can't see Africa, so I'll bring it to her. I feel so blessed to have met Trista, and I'm filled with the excitement of getting to know her better. Now, we just have to see where it may lead. It doesn't take long before I return to the hospital to bring her back to the hotel.

"So, are you ready to go?" I ask.

With a sigh of relief, she answers, "You bet I am. Don't get me wrong… the staff's been great here, but I don't think anyone would like to spend a vacation in a foreign hospital."

"Well, Miss Trista, no more hospitals for you. I've already moved your belongings to the spare room in my suite, so everything's ready for you."

"Are you sure about this, Phil?"

"Yes, I'm sure. I want to help you and take care of you. Are you okay with me helping you?"

"Yeah, I guess. I just don't want to be a pain."

"Enough of that already. Trista, meeting you has been the highlight of my trip. This is just a way to keep it going a little longer," I admit.

I notice her blush and tear up a little. I adore how such a small gesture of admiration gets to her. I can't wait to learn more about why. I get her a wheelchair and take her down to the driver, who I have waiting outside the hospital. I hope that she doesn't feel obligated to stay with me. This should be a great opportunity to bond and really get to know the woman who has entered my heart. As we drive through the streets of Tanzania, I see her eyes light up, seeing the locals go about their day. I hope to have the opportunity to show her so much more. I want to experience Africa through her eyes, with such hope and promise. Before long, we're back at the hotel, and Trista insists on walking in.

"Well, here we are. This is my... *our* suite. Welcome." I slide the key card through until it clicks, and I swing open the door for her.

"Oh, what have you done, Phil? This is amazing!" She gushes at the sight of the flower-filled room.

"I want you to experience Africa, even if just from a hotel." I smile at her reaction.

Trista slowly walks... no, hobbles around the room. She leans in and examines every bunch of flowers, smelling them. "These are so beautiful."

"I have another surprise." Walking beside her, I take her hand in mine and lead her to the dining room. The hotel staff's done a wonderful job, and the entire feast is laid out for her picking.

"Phil, this is way too much!"

"Nothing's too much for you."

"But you really don't even know me," she adds.

"That may be true, but I hope to learn so much about you. I was so lucky to have Sara in my life, but I lost her without showing her every moment of every day what she meant to me. I never thought I'd get another chance at happiness again. Then I met you and realized that it's possible. Now, I'm not saying I love you, but I'm experiencing feelings like never before. I want to examine these feelings, and see where they may lead. I also never want to take advantage of the time I have, I've already learned that tomorrow is never promised. Are you up to exploring this with me?" I attempt to backtrack my words a little, realizing I don't want to come on too strong.

She takes a seat, hands covering her mouth. I can tell she's surprised by my admission. I had to tell her though; I had to put myself out there for her.

"Phil, I have never experienced love before, at least not true love like you had with Sara. You make me feel like a princess, and I, too, have feelings for you. It's almost as if fate is throwing us together and saying, 'how can you miss this?' I'd love to stay and get to know you better, get to see us together. My only fear is that we both go home in a little over a week and what then? We live on opposite ends of the country."

I take a seat next to her; taking her hand in mine and I kiss it. "We can figure that out later. For now, let's just enjoy each other and this wonderful meal."

The Climb

The meal the hotel set up for us is amazing. The large oak table is filled from one end to the other with fruits and various cuisines from around Africa. Some of the dishes I recognize, others I don't. One dish I recognize from a menu I read is called 'Bunny Chow'; a hollowed-out loaf of bread filled with curry. Another is zebra sausage... and yes, they actually eat zebra here. We both try a little of everything. Some is good, but some can stay here in Africa for the locals. Not everything works with our taste buds. This is exactly what I wanted... to experience Africa... and food is always a good way to do that. Once we finish our own *Taste of Africa*, I help Trista get settled and comfortable in her bedroom before the spa staff comes in. I want her to relax, and what better way than a full spa treatment right in your room!

"Phil, this really is too much. You're spoiling me," she insists.

I smile, admitting, "I know, just trying to impress you." A small chuckle slips out, "I enjoy it. I haven't had anyone to spoil in a while, so you're getting all my pent-up spoiling."

"Fair enough, I'll stop complaining and enjoy. Thank you again. You're far too good to me."

"It really is my pleasure. Maybe when you're done we can watch a movie together."

"I'd love that."

I leave her to her pampering and pull out my laptop. After all that time on Kilimanjaro, I should check my e-mail. I can see that my assistant has really been keeping up on things during my absence. She was a great hire; I think she'll be an asset to the company.

Now that I've attended to a few work issues, I decide to throw on a pot of coffee. I hope that Trista's up to a night of hanging out.

After a few hours, the door to the room down the hall opens and Trista starts to hobble out. She's wearing a large terrycloth bathrobe, with her hair piled on top of her head in a messy bun. I struggle to regain my breath, as I've never seen a more beautiful sight. I rush over to her and sweep her up in my arms, fighting the urge to rip the robe from her shapely body. "Did you enjoy getting pampered?"

"Oh, it was so amazing, Phil. I've never had a massage or a facial. Actually, I've never had a pedicure or manicure, either. I understand why some women insist on going to the spa all the time. Thank you so much."

"You're welcome. As I mentioned earlier, I'm hoping we could just sit around and watch movies. Maybe get to know each other even more. If you feel up to it, that is."

"Absolutely, I'm so energized now." She beams.

I walk over to the large sectional in the living area and sit her in the corner so that she is lying across the sofa. I already have some fluffy pillows and a blanket ready for her, so I cover her up and hand her the pay-per-view list. "Why don't you look through the movies available. I have another surprise for you."

She looks up at me with her big, emerald-green eyes. "Phil, really, you've done more than enough for me."

"I'll be right back, trust me." I let out a small smile.

I return with Bernard, the suites butler. He's wheeling a large silver tray that is covered by an equally large silver cover. "Okay, dessert time," I announce, with a grin.

Bernard lifts the lid, revealing various types of ice cream, fruit, brownies, sauces, and candies; everything we need for a sundae overdose. "Hope you like sweets." I take a seat next to her.

"Well, I can definitely go for some ice cream."

Bernard helps to make our sundaes with everything we like. Both Trista and I sit back and enjoy the nice treat before settling on a movie and relaxing. I want everything to be perfect for her, to show her what it's like to be the sunshine in someone's day. That's what she is to me. She lights up my entire day.

Chapter 7

Trista

I think I'm going to have to take up regular spa days. Phil's shown me what it's like to be a woman. Pampering oneself should be mandatory. I have spent my entire life just going through the motions, trying to please everyone but myself. After university, I took on menial, low-income jobs, making barely enough to survive. This lifestyle Phil's introducing me to, makes me want to better myself. Maybe I can take some business classes once I return home. My BA hasn't really done much for me, but I can use it to advance into some other courses in University. It's about time I start enjoying my life and living for something, not just surviving. Life is so much more and I'm finally realizing it.

This trip's teaching me more than I could've ever hoped for. It's time to move on from my personal assistant job at the bank and take control of my life. In the eight years that I've been at the bank, I have hated every moment of it. Mr. Pollack, my boss, is a pompous ass, never thinking of anyone but himself. I'm surprised wife number five has lasted three years already. It burns right through me, knowing that he makes over a million dollars a year when I barely make forty grand. I know he works hard, but I work equally as hard. I deserve a life like this; a life like what Phil is showing me. I'm happy with some parts of my life though. I have a great two-bedroom apartment and a few good friends. I enjoy staying to myself and my friends accept that, as long as I join them at least one Tuesday a month for wings and beer.

For now though, at least for the next few days, I vow to allow myself to let go. I'll open up to Phil and let him know the real me. He's treated me better in one week than anyone has ever treated me before. I can't help but wonder where this may lead. I know that my feelings are growing for him, but I wonder if he feels the same, or if he's nothing more than a kind soul. I realize he's admitted to feeling something; it's just difficult for me to believe that a man like him wants me. With the passion he has shown me when we kissed, it's hard to believe it's not real, even while fighting my insecurities. I'd love for this to last.

"What are ya thinkin' about, Trista?" Phil asks.

"Oh, just about how wonderful this trip's been, believe it or not. Despite hurting myself, I'm learning more about myself and having more fun on this trip than any other time in my life," I admit.

"I am too. Can I admit something to you? I don't want you to think I'm crazy."

"Phil, you can tell me anything. One thing you need to know is, I try not to judge others, so please, share away."

"Well, from the first day on Kili, I knew you were different... you were special. I felt things for you almost immediately. I never believed in love at first sight, but I can't help but wonder now. I know this must sound insane, but I think Sara may have brought us together. There's a spark I can't deny."

I smile nervously. "That's not crazy, Phil. I'm flattered, and I must admit that I, too, have felt something between us. I'm looking forward to learning more about what this is."

Phil moves from his spot on the sofa and sits right next to me, looking at me with deep passion in his eyes. Leaning forward, his soft lips touch mine ever so gently, and then he pulls back. Phil's hand brushes through the loose strands of my hair, as he looks deep into my eyes. I lift my head so that our lips meet again, moving together in unison. Feeling fire surge through my entire body, unlike anything I've ever felt before. I yearn for him; I want him like I have never wanted anyone before.

"Phil, I want you, but I can't. I have to tell you something."

With a concerned look, Phil responds, "I'm sorry. Do you have someone back home? I didn't mean to be so presumptuous."

"No, it's not that. See... well... I've never been with anyone before. I've only had one serious boyfriend and we never took it to that level. So now, I guess I just figured that... I've waited this long... well, I figure I might as well wait until... until marriage. I never meant to lead you on. I'm so sorry."

"Trista, there is nothing to be sorry about. I admire you for your choice. Do you mind if I just hold you while we watch the movie?"

"I'd like that very much." I smile, with a sense of relief.

Phil lays down next to me, holding me close. I can feel the ripples of his frame on my back. I drift off to sleep in the comfort of his arms, as we watch 'The Wedding Singer,' only to wake the following morning in my bed. I assume Phil carried me in here because I don't remember waking. I look around my large room but see no sign of Phil. I wonder if he slept in his own room. I also wonder if he's still interested in me, now that he knows my big, dark secret. Shaking the thoughts from my head, I dress and hobble out to the main room, still amazed by the beauty of Phil's suite. The large room is filled with the flowers he surprised me with upon my arrival, and the strong aroma of coffee and fresh fruit fill the air. Making my way to the dining area, I pause when I see Phil standing there, sipping on his steaming cup of java.

"Good morning, beautiful. I took the liberty of ordering room service. Can I offer you a cup of coffee?"

"That would be great, thanks."

"So, how are you feeling today? Would you be up for a little outing?"

"Oh, hell yeah! What do you have in mind?" I stir a spoonful of sugar and a dollop of cream into my coffee, and take a big breath in, basking in the aroma. God, have I missed good coffee.

"I was hoping we could go on a safari. It should be easy enough for you; we just sit in the jeep most of the time."

"Really? A safari? I'd love that, thank you so much."

"I hope you don't mind, but I ordered you a proper outfit." He hands me a large box.

Looking at the large white box in front of me, I excitedly lift the lid. Moving the tissue paper off to the side, I peer inside. I find myself staring at the nicest safari outfit, ever. The light-colored khaki material is so soft. The pants and jacket are covered with plenty of pockets. The leg is zippered, to fit over my cast; he really does think of everything. I'm so excited about going out today.

"Can I assume by the look on your face that you like the outfit? I know it's nothing spectacular, but it's necessary for our safari."

Smiling back at him, I admit, "I love it! This is exactly like what you see in the movies. I can't wait!"

"Well then, eat up and let's get ready. Our driver will be here in an hour." Phil pulls out a chair and sits next to me after kissing the top of my head.

Before long, Phil's leading me to the car that's waiting for us in front of the hotel. I feel a sense of belonging as we snuggle together in the back seat, his arm around me and my head cuddled into his broad shoulder. We just kinda fit together. The hour drive to the safari resort seems to fly by, and before we realize it, we're there. The small huts all have jeeps parked in front of them. Phil enters one of the huts to finalize arrangements, as I enjoy the beauty surrounding me. The land reaches as far as the eye can see. Dry, warm air surrounds me and I feel happiness. In the distance, I can see a few trees and hear the call of the animals, I'm excited for the adventure ahead.

    The sun's high in the sky, beyond the most amazing meadow. The umbrella throne trees line the horizon, and the sight's breathtaking. Dust flies through the air as the wild zebras run by. When you see pictures of Africa, this is exactly what you expect. The only difference is, it's not a picture... I'm really here and experiencing this, first hand. I could never imagine such beauty before.

    "Did you know that every zebra has a different pattern of stripes?" Phil walks out of the little hut.

    "I had no clue, that's very interesting."

    "I thought so too. I read it in a National Geographic magazine one time. So, are you ready? Our tour guide will be out shortly."

    Phil leads me towards a beige colored jeep.

Chapter 8

Phil

The jeep takes us over the rough terrain of a red rock path, with tall green grass lining the roadway, giving the perfect contrast. Picturesque trees and bushes are everywhere, various animals running wild and free, the beauty of nature's creations surrounding us; it's all so remarkable, yet still cannot compare to the woman sitting next to me. I don't think I've ever respected a woman as much as I respect her. Nor have I ever longed to be with a woman more. I want to make the most of the few days we have left together and make them memorable for both of us. The tour guide explains to us about the indigenous people of Africa and takes us to an area with about a dozen little mud huts.

"Jambo," one lady says.

"Jambo," we greet back, remembering that it means hello.

"Hey Phil, do you remember that song they sang while climbing Kili?" Trista asks.

"Jambo, Jambo Bwana," I chuckle. "I love that song. It has so much spirit and just helped to push us through."

"Yeah, you know even with fracturing my foot, this has been the best time of my life. I really owe that to you."

"To me?" I say, taken aback.

"Yeah, you never let me give up. Thanks to you, I made it to the summit, and now here."

"Well, I'm glad to have someone as stunning as you to share all this with." I lean in for a small kiss.

A dark African woman invites us into her hut. Inside, seven kids sit around the small, single room. The eldest child looks to be about ten. She stands and waves for us to sit. Another child comes with a cup of tea. Both Trista and I look at the guide for assurance that it's safe to drink. With a slight nod and a smile, we both take a sip. I open up my backpack, and pull out handfuls of candy for the family, as well as a pouch of rice and dried beans for the mother. With tears, she hugs and thanks me. Warmth fills me, as I understand how such a small amount of food will help this family. I notice Trista wipe a tear from her eye.

"You really are an amazing man, Phil. I believe you thought of everything. This family will never forget what you've done for them."

"Well, then I guess I should hand out enough for the entire village." I go to the jeep and pull off one of four large metal bunkers, and the tour guide helps me carry it to the center of the village, in the midst of all the huts.

As the families all rush out to see, I motion to Trista to open it, and she lifts the lid to display enough food to sustain the village for at least a month. The women all bow down to us with tears and screams of joy, knowing their babies will all be fed. I'm so happy to witness such elation and to see that Trista feels the same as I do. After a tour of the area, we reload into the jeep and continue on our way.

"That was remarkable, Phil. When did you even have time to arrange this? I can't wait to see what's next." Her smile can compete with the light of the moon.

"I called ahead to order it. I wanted to make sure we help those we visit. Next, we are off to a giraffe farm."

"What? I never knew there was such a thing."

"Yeah, it sounds great. We'll get to be face to face with the giraffes."

The tour guide looks over his shoulder. "Twiga farm to the right."

"Twiga?" we both question.

"Yeah man, Twiga... ah... giraffe farm."

We look to our right and see dozens of twigas, as they call them, running across the wide-open land.

The tour guide leads us up an old wooden staircase. There are about twenty steep steps, so I help Trista because of her cast. Every step we take, a creaking sound comes from the wood, and we both grip the handrail just a little tighter. Not that it would save us from a collapse... I guess it's nothing more than a false sense of security. The stairs lead us to around wooden hut that's high above the ground. It's simple, but there are tables set up for lunch and a balcony to view the wildlife. I can tell Trista's wiped out from climbing the stairs. Helping her to a table and pulling out a chair, I lift her injured leg up to rest. The small staff at the giraffe farm begins to bring out a traditional African lunch for us.

"I'm completely blown away; I never knew they had stuff like this here in Africa. How on earth did you ever find it, Phil?"

The Climb

"My boss had told me about all the great things to do while here. His wife lived here for nearly ten years before they met. So, I had a plan to do his top ten suggestions."

"I'm sorry. I must really be holding you back." She starts to play with her food.

"I don't want to hear you talk like that. I enjoy being with you. The time we're spending together is great. You've actually helped me achieve one of his top ten, one I never expected to accomplish," I admit, without letting on that she helped me to fall in love; my boss's number one activity in Africa. He met his wife while he was here on vacation; they've never been apart since. She was working at a marathon he'd enrolled in. He stopped for water and never started the race again. He told me he had always been running to find something, maybe himself, he never knew. Until he found her... that's when he knew he didn't have to run anymore.

After Trista and I finish eating, we go to the balcony and watch the giraffes. The tour guide gives us some snacks to feed the animals, and they eat right from our hands, lapping up the treats with their big black tongues. The guide then takes a treat, places it in his mouth and leans slightly over the edge. A giraffe walks right to him and takes the treat right from his lips.

"That's the coolest thing I've ever seen." Trista beams with excitement.

"Here, why don't we try? We can get pictures." I hand her another treat. She places it between her lips and leans forward. A smaller giraffe comes toward her mouth, opens wide, and licks her face, taking the treat right from between her lips.

"EEEWWWW, that was so gross and so cool at the same time. His tongue is so rough, like sandpaper." She giggles.

"I got some great shots, look at these." I turn the digital camera her way and flip through the pictures. These are priceless; her face scrunches up as the animal gets closer. We both laugh at the expressions in the photos.

Before long, Trista and I are taking refuge in the back of the jeep, and we are on the road again. Driving through the area, we're at the actual safari by three. The various wild animals are running free around us; I'm amazed when a lion begins to follow the jeep. Trista pulls out her camera and snaps a few photos of the king of the jungle, who's within feet of us.

"Miss. Trista, Mr. Phil, it is difficult to see but if you look at the umbrella tree in the distance, you can see a leopard on the first branch," our tour guide informs us.

"Oh wow, that's fantastic," Trista says with excitement.

I look at the woman next to me. "You're the most beautiful thing I have ever seen. I mean, *that's* amazing."

By, Charlotte Blackwell

Leaning in, I softly touch my lips to hers; there's a faint taste of strawberry from her lip gloss. Her lips are like satin, so soft and smooth, as mine move along with hers. Lifting my hand from the small of her back then slowly brushing across her check, I realize I'm so in love with her. Our kiss continues as we sit in the back of the jeep, the lion close behind us. Suddenly, the vehicle hits a big bump, and Trista flies off the edge of the jeep to the ground.

"STOP!" I scream.

The driver slams on the brakes and looks back as I'm already jumping down to her aid. The lion closing in on us has a hunger in his eyes I have never seen. I race to get Trista up, but she's unconscious and the cast makes her even more awkward to handle. Our guide leaps from the jeep to help me.

"Mr. Phil, we must hurry. The lion is hungry and preparing to pounce. You see he is circling and marking his territory."

"Get her legs, I've got her head." I throw my arms under her arms, wrapping them around her chest. We lift her into the back of the jeep and jump in as the lion lunges for us. A blood-curdling scream comes from over my shoulder. I turn to see the lion has our tour guide by the ankle.

"Mr. Phil, please help me!" The pain evident in his voice.

My heart's pounding through my chest, adrenaline kicking in. I dig through the equipment stored in the back seat and find a walking stick. With a good grip, I begin to beat the lion. He releases his grip on our guide and roars, so fierce the jeep shakes. The guide pulls himself into the jeep, putting it into gear and flooring it. Driving away, I lean over to look at his injury.

"My friend, allow me to drive. You're injured; just tell me where to go." I see his left foot barely hanging on. "You need a tourniquet for your wound."

"Yes, I think I need help. Just drive to the next turn-off, and there will be a medic station there," he instructs.

Being far enough away from the lion, he pulls over. I take a rope from the back and assist him in tying it below the knee of his left leg. Falling to the side, our guide begins to seize, going into shock. I know I must hurry and get Trista and our guide to the medic. I slam the jeep into gear and hammer down on the accelerator, driving as fast as I can through the rough terrain without jarring my injured passengers. The jeep kicks up dust and rocks behind us. A moan erupts from the back seat and glancing over my shoulder, I see Trista stirring.

"Trista baby, just lay still. You fell off the jeep and were unconscious. I'm getting you to the medic. I'm so sorry baby; I should've never brought you out here."

"Phil... uh, I don't..." She begins to vomit.

I know that she's not well, "Almost there baby, just around this corner." I take the turn and see the medic station ahead. It's only taken about five minutes, yet it has seemed like an hour. I maneuver the jeep up to the door, kicking up dust around us and honking the horn; the staff inside run out to see what the commotion is.

I shout as I get out of the jeep. "I have two injured, both lost consciousness. The woman fell off the moving jeep and hit her head. Our guide was attacked by a lion. I've placed a tourniquet on his leg, but he seized. I think both are in shock."

The team helps to load the two into the station, and begin their examination. Another staff member interviews me and a conservation officer goes to check on the animal. I explained the area and he nods with acknowledgment. He assures me I did the right thing, and explains that since the lion has attacked a human, he may need to be monitored for further aggressive behavior.

"You were very brave; the lion is the king of the jungle and could have killed you all," he announces, before leaving.

I watch from afar, as the medical team works on our guide and Trista. I'm drenched in sweat from the heat and my anxiety. I pray that Trista's okay... I can't believe she's been hurt again. I should've never brought her out here. I think I may have pushed things too far for her. Pacing back and forth across the white floor of the station, I can't help but regret the danger I put her in.

By, Charlotte Blackwell

Chapter 9

Trista

wake to strangers hovering around me. Not knowing how I got here, I begin to worry. Hearing Phil's voice in the background calms me.

"So, you are sure she'll be alright?" Phil asks.

"Yes sir, your wife will be fine. There is only a mild concussion," a female voice informs.

"She's not my... ah, thank you so much. I really appreciate your help," he mutters.

I let out a small chuckle and they all turn to me. Phil's at my side in seconds.

"Trista baby, I'm so sorry."

"What happened?"

"Well, we were kissing and hit a bump in the road. You fell off the jeep and were nearly attacked by a lion. You hit your head and have a concussion," he explains.

"So then, why are you sorry? It doesn't sound like you did anything wrong."

"It just seems like you keep getting hurt around me. I probably shouldn't have brought you on a safari while your leg is still injured. Maybe we should've done something a little less dangerous."

"Phil, you can stop that talk right now! You've done more for me than anyone ever has in all my life. I've enjoyed our outing and want to continue with your plan. I'm fine, nothing more than a headache."

"Trista, you amaze me. Well, I think the medics are going to release you soon. We are getting a new tour guide, as ours is being taken in for surgery. But I think it's best if we go back to the hotel." Phil continues to explain how our guide helped save me but got caught in the cross fire. I feel terrible and am very concerned. I insist they keep us informed on how he's doing, and the staff agrees.

Before long, the medics come and examine me again and they agree that I can leave. When the new guide arrives, we decide to call it a day and return to the hotel. The guide drives us back; it takes nearly two hours by the time we get to Phil's room. He helps me in, lifting me in his arms, and carries me to the sofa.

"Rest here for a few minutes; I'll go run a bath for you." Phil smiles and adds, "we can prop your cast on the side of the tub."

"Thanks, Phil. That sounds great."

Phil turns on some music and heads to the washroom. The sound of the tub filling echoes down the hall, and the room fills with the scent of vanilla. He must've added some bubbles, I think to myself. The water shuts off and there's a knock at the door, Phil comes running out of the washroom.

"Don't move, I got it," he shouts, as he runs past me. Being very secretive, he comes back and says, "Okay, why don't I help you get into the bath."

"Thanks, Phil, but really, I'm okay. I can do it."

"Well, let me just help you get in there and you can relax some more."

Sweeping me up in his arms from the sofa, Phil carries me to the bathroom and places me on the small, white vanity stool. Kneeling in front of me, he starts to pull off the sock from my uninjured foot.

"Phil, I'm okay, I can really do this on my own."

"Trista, don't be so stubborn. It will be difficult to get into the tub with your cast. I promise not to look," he insists while handing me a large, white towel as he smiles.

I take the towel and hold it over myself. Phil unzips the side of the specially made khaki pants he gave me and helps slide them off. Slowly running his hand down the bare flesh of my thigh, tingles explode down my entire leg. Phil sits on his heels, looking at me, my pants in his hand. The look in his eyes fills me with passion. The feelings I'm having for him begin to overtake my thoughts. He sits up on his knees; reaching behind the towel, he lifts my shirt over my head. My hands tangled in the shirt, he holds them above my head and leans in for a kiss. The towel falls to my lap, as the kiss becomes more passionate. Phil leans closer and presses me against the wall. My heart beats faster with every passing moment, wanting him more than I've ever wanted anyone before. I press into him, yearning for him, wanting more, needing more. As he pulls my hands free from my shirt, I wrap my arms around him. Slowly our lips part and I let out a sigh.

"Okay beautiful, it's time to get you into the bath."

By, Charlotte Blackwell

I pull the towel up again and reach behind my back, unsnapping the clasp on my bra. I slip one arm out and then the other, tossing the bra off to the side. Phil reaches under the towel grasping both sides of my panties, slowly sliding them down. I let out a small giggle, and he smiles. With the towel strategically wrapped around me, he lifts me off the vanity stool and places me in the bath, casted leg resting on the edge over a folded towel.

"Thanks for everything, Phil." I smile, trying to forget that he's seen me in just my under garments seconds ago.

"You're thanking me? I seem to keep making things worse for you."

"No, you've shown me things I never knew existed. I can see that kindness still does exist in some people."

"Well, now it's time for me to show you relaxation. I have a few things to deal with, but I'll come back to check on you in a few minutes," Phil says, leaning down to kiss my head.

I lay back in the tub, taking in the alluring scent of vanilla. I was too caught up in Phil before to notice that he had candles going all around me. He really does know how to make a girl feel special. Closing my eyes, I begin to reflect on the past week and how so much has happened since I first landed in Tanzania. I only have another week here; seven more days with the man I'm falling in love with. I don't want it to end, but I have to get back to my life, and he needs to get back to his. I can't let another moment pass me by. I've waited to share myself with someone I love, and now that I've found him, I will not miss this chance. Tonight, I'll give myself to the man I love for the first time.

With my eyes closed, imagining being in Phil's arms. I hear something and open my eyes. I see Phil setting a bottle of champagne down with a tray of chocolate dipped strawberries. I watch as he fills a glass, but he hasn't noticed my eyes are open and continues to move with great stealth. As he turns to place the glass of champagne by my side, I reach up and grab his hand. Looking down at me, he smiles and leans down for a kiss. Giving him just a little tug, he falls right into the tub with me, the bubbled water splashing around us. We both let out a laugh.

"What are you doing?" Phil sputters and kisses me.

"I thought you could use a bath too, and now that you are already in here, well... you may as well join me." I smile and begin to lift his now soaked shirt off.

"But Trista, you said... I don't want to... well, I want to respect your wishes, but if I get in the bath with you..."

"Phil, I know what I said, but I want you to join me. Whatever happens, happens. You make me want to live life to the fullest and I don't want to pass up something I may regret missing."

I toss his wet shirt to the floor, and he stands to remove his wet trousers. His boxer briefs cling to his skin, showing every asset. He brings the strawberries and champagne to the side table on the tub and removes his shorts to join me. Even in this amazing moment, he takes great care not to bump my leg.

"I've had the best week of my life. Thank you so much for showing me how to live life and enjoy every moment of it."

"Trista, you've shown me that I can love again. I think you're even showing me what true love is, the kind of love you just feel without fully knowing what you're getting into. Don't get me wrong, I loved Sara, but you... you are special."

"Love... you..." I'm flustered and my heart is nearly pounding through my chest.

"In case you haven't noticed, I'm in love with you," he repeats and presses his lips to mine as he smiles at his admission.

Sitting across from one another in the oversized tub, we continue to kiss with such passion. Phil runs his fingertips over my bare shoulder, wiping the bubbles away. He moves so that he is sitting behind me, cradling me in his arms. I lean back on his bare, rippled chest and abs. Our skin touching like this is like a fire burning out of control.

Phil slowly rubs my shoulders and runs his hands around to my front. I take a deep breath and relax into his arms. Feeling soft kisses along the nape of my neck, my back twists as his lips move over me. Tilting my head back so that our lips can meet, we kiss. Taking one of the strawberries in my fingers, I run it over my lips, then move the berry to his mouth and he takes a bite. I finish the berry and take a sip of champagne.

"Trista, I don't think I can handle this much longer," he pants

"Nor can I. Maybe we should move somewhere more comfortable," I suggest.

By, Charlotte Blackwell

Chapter 10

Phil

I wrap one of the robes around myself, and help Trista out of the bath, taking another robe and covering her with it. Pressing my lips to hers, I lift her into my arms and carry her to my room. Laying her gently on the king size bed, I reach for the remote and turn on the large white fireplace. The flames cast a soft orange glow around the room. Leaning over the bed, I begin to kiss Trista's body as I remove the robe from her. I'm slow in my motions, both to respect her and to enjoy every moment.

"Just relax; I want this to be special and enjoyable for you. Let me know if at any time you're uncomfortable."

"I... I... okay." She lets out a sigh of relief.

Smiling at her nervousness, I run my hands along her arms and intertwine my fingers with hers. Pressing my body next to hers, I feel the blood rushing through me. Passionately, our lips move as one, and I move her arms over her head. Running my hands back down her sides and placing them on her hips, I slowly slide down her toned, fit, and perfectly proportioned body.

"You are so beautiful."

"I don't understand what you see in me," she whispers.

"Are you doing okay? You sure you want to do this?" I ask with concern.

Her good leg wraps around my back, and I feel it tugging the bathrobe off of me. The smoothness of her shapely leg rubs down my back, her heel resting between my shoulders and mid back. With need increasing in me, I slip my hands under her, pulling her closer; I can feel her heart pounding. She lifts her hips into me, confirming the depth of her enjoyment. Her hand moves to my hair, and she tangles it through her fingers.

"Phil, I can't handle this anymore. I want you... I need you. Please, Phil, make love to me." The passion and need is evident in her voice.

"I want to make love to you more than anything. I want to feel you, feel every part of you. I want to be the only man to ever make love to you."

With complete love for her, I press my mouth to hers and take her in. Intertwining my fingers with hers, I move her arms above her head. Never have I felt as much passion as I do now; embracing me, taking me to a place I never expected.

For the next hour, it's as though we're the only two people in the world. She's everything I could ever want. "Phil, I... I... I'm glad it was you," she whispers.

"I am too." I move next to her and hold her close as we fall asleep in each other's arms.

Waking the following morning, I find myself wanting to make love to Trista again. Spending the entire day in bed with her would be a dream, but I have other plans. We're only here for a few more days, and I want it to be memorable for both of us. Not knowing what will come of this, or where life will lead us, I believe it's important to make the best of the time we do have together. Deciding to leave her sleep, I pull the plush white duvet over her and proceed to the large ensuite. Pausing for a moment in the doorway, I turn and look at the women in my bed. I never noticed how beautiful this room actually was until now. I can't help but wonder if it is Trista that makes it so beautiful. Sleeping peacefully, I notice the shiny, auburn-brown color of her hair draped over the pillow; a natural color I've never seen before. Her soft, plump lips with slightly upturned corners make her look so sweet. She looks happy and at peace, laying on the bed.

Once I collect myself and turn back to the washroom, I close the large French doors and start the shower. Once the glass door steams up, I jump in, allowing the water to rush over me. I think I may need to get a shower like this at home; the five showerheads spraying in all directions is both relaxing and refreshing. As I lather the soap and wash myself, I feel the nerves strike me. Trista and I have gotten to know one another so well, yet I still have no idea of where this will lead or if it will end. I can only hope she enjoys my last attempt to show her the sites of Africa. I wonder if she likes helicopters.

After dressing, I go out to the living room and order room service. The knock on the door wakes Trista and she hobbles out of the room wearing the bathrobe from last night.

"You ordered breakfast? Thank you."

"I thought you might be hungry after all the physical activity you got last night," I joke, as I walk over to her and kiss her. "How are you feeling today?"

"I'm doing great. Thank you for last night. I couldn't imagine it being any better."

"You don't know how happy that makes me. I was nervous that you'd think we made a mistake."

"No Phil, like I said, I'm glad it was you. I'm just a little sad that this is all ending soon."

"It doesn't have to. Why don't you come to New York with me?" I smile.

"As much as I'd love that, I can't. I have a job and a condo in San Francisco. I have responsibilities."

"Just promise me that this isn't the end of us. I want you in my life. I know it will be hard living on opposite coasts, but we can travel to visit each other."

"Of course, I wouldn't want it any other way."

Deciding that we no longer want to think of the inevitable, we sit down at the large dining room table to enjoy our meal together. I inform her to prepare for a day of excitement and wonder. Before long, she's dressed and ready to go. I wrap a black cloth over her eyes, blindfolding her. I lead her to the roof of our hotel, taking the small staircase outside our penthouse suite. A chopper's waiting for us, and with the *swoosh* of the propeller, Trista's hair flies around her face and I remove the blindfold.

"Oh my God! Are you kidding me?" She wraps her arms around my neck with excitement.

"I figured we best try something a little less adventurous today. So, I've arranged for a helicopter tour of the area. I hope you're alright with this."

"Yes, of course! It's always been a dream of mine to take a ride in one, and to tour Africa in it… with you… this will make it unforgettable."

Trista takes my hand as I help her into the chopper, and the pilot hands us each a headset. Reaching over Trista, I help to secure her harness. The whooshing of the propeller speeds up as we lift from the ground, shifting from side to side as it steadies in the air. The wind rushes through each side and swirls around us, allowing the fresh, unpolluted air to enter our lungs. The smells of all the trees and soil overtake each and every breath we take. What could be better than this? She wraps her arms around my bicep, holding on. I sense a little fear in her touch. I want her to feel safe and secure, so I place my hand over her lap, holding her knees next to mine and keeping her close.

The sky's slightly overcast, but every so often, the brilliant blue peeks through the clouds. The land beneath us is dry and pale brown, with lush green trees everywhere. Then, over a hill of green grass and shrubs, the world below changes before our eyes. A large river runs along the side of the hill, with grand canyons and waterfalls that pour down to the river below; a beautiful sight to see and to share with the woman I love. The water, so clear, it's almost transparent, misting up into the air as it hits the rocks below. A large brilliant rainbow reaches from one end of the canyon to the other. A flawless sight for a perfect day.

I point out of the side of the chopper. "Do you see that?"

"Yes! Oh my god, look at the baby elephant following behind its mom. Look how it holds Mom's tails as they walk. He's so cute."

As we continue to fly over a cliff, there is suddenly a large canyon of red rock. We fly lower down so that we are surrounded by the land. As the chopper rises back up, we enjoy the sights of the pumas, the hippos and many other animals frolicking in their natural habitat. The pilot begins to make his descent on to the top of a mountainous landscape. We land on a high peak and are surrounded by canyons, so we're able to see the majority of the land below. As the landing skids touch the ground and the *whooshing* sound slows, he turns to us with a smile.

"We locals call this 'God's Window.' It has the most amazing view of Africa you will ever experience. The land stretches as far as the eye can see. I have a picnic here for you and will return in ninety minutes to collect you. Please enjoy."

I place a blanket in the tall, uncut grass, only twenty feet away from the edge of the cliff, giving us a perfect view and a place to relax. The tall rocks, resembling Stonehenge, give us the perfect amount of shade now that the sky's clear blue again and the sun is shining. The wildflowers around us emit a beautiful bouquet of scents. Opening the basket, we find an assortment of fine cheeses, caviar, crackers, and fruit. We both savor the meal before us, and I pour us each a glass of wine.

"Thank you so much for the past few days, Phil. I still can't believe everything you've done for me. It almost feels like I'm in a movie," Trista says with elation.

"Trista, I want to shower you with memories like this for the rest of our lives. You deserve this and so much more." I smile at the woman beside me, knowing that my heart has finally found peace.

Relaxing in each other's arms while sharing some wine makes an amazing memory we can hold together forever. We cap it off with some wonderful conversation; tiny details about our childhoods, schools, and jobs. Trying to learn everything we can about one another. Before long, ninety minutes have passed, and our ride comes back for us, as promised. This has been an experience, I'll never forget.

Chapter 11

Trista

It's our final night together and I don't want to leave the suite for any reason. I'm not sure when we'll see each other again, but I hope it's not too long. We both agree that we'll make arrangements once we get back to the States.

"Trista, you can come in now," Phil calls from the master bedroom.

I slowly walk towards the room, wondering what he has up his sleeve this time. He refused to let me in the room after we came back from dinner tonight. Making my way through the long-marbled hallway, I reach the frosted French doors to the suite and open them. Phil's standing in the doorway. I look at the man I've fallen for and he smiles, his eyes not moving from mine. I can see the passion and love behind his gaze. His smile, warm and welcoming. I move towards him and meet his lips with my own. Fire ignites with each swipe of his tongue against mine until slowly, we part.

"Trista, you've shown me so much these past few weeks, now I want to show you one last time how a woman should be treated. Please come and join me in our room." He takes my hand in his and leads me in.

The large room is aglow with hundreds of candles, leading all the way out to the balcony. Champagne and fondue are set up on the table outside. I'm rendered speechless by this beautiful sight, including the moon and stars above that sparkle like diamonds. Phil pulls the chair out from the table and guides me into my seat, lifting the cloth napkin and placing it in my lap. He smiles and looks back to the table. My eyes follow his, and I see a long velvet box.

"This is something to remember me by." Phil takes the box and opens it before me. A white gold chain, with a beautiful diamond-encrusted circle pendant, is presented to me. "This circle represents us, and what I hope is to come; that our two worlds have met and will continue to meet for eternity. I've fallen for you so completely in such a short time and want you to know that I love you... and always will."

I begin to cry, not knowing what the future holds for us. "Thank you so much, Phil. Will you please help me put it on?"

He removes the necklace from the box, opens the clasp, and places it around my neck. Tiny kisses from his lips run up and down my throat, as he slips the spaghetti strap of my dress off my shoulder and continues to kiss me all over. As usual, the fireworks go off inside of me until I can't take it anymore. I pull him in front of me and pull his light blue V-neck t-shirt over his head. Admiring his flawless pecs and abs, I run my hands down the perfectly formed muscles. Leaning forward, I press my lips to his skin, kissing the amazing man before me. He pulls me up around his waist, my broken leg dangling over his forearm. Our bodies press firmly against each other, as he carries me back to the bed we've shared the past few nights.

"God, Trista, I never want to leave. I want you in my arms forever," he sighs, as he places me on the bed.

"I wish we didn't have to leave. I wish I wasn't going home tomorrow."

Phil's hands slide seamlessly down my body, pulling the black lace panties from my legs. He stands at the end of the bed and allows his pants to drop to the floor. I never realized how beautiful the male body was. He moves up the bed, hovering over me, and the touch of his skin against mine sends me over the edge. Once he reaches my lips and touches his to mine, I grab his shoulders, roll him over and sit on top of him.

"Tonight's your turn to experience everything. Just let me know if I do anything wrong." I'm sure that doesn't sound sexy, but being that Phil's my first, my inexperience is bound to show. I just want to make sure I can please him.

"Trista, you don't have to do anything, I get pleasure from pleasing you."

"Oh my god, Trista... that was amazing. I don't know how you make me feel this way, but I love it," he says, with bated breath.

"I guess that means I did alright?" I smirk.

"Oh, you did amazing. Now that I'm warmed up, you had better be ready, because you are not leaving this bed until your plane leaves. Honestly, I might not even let you go then."

I can't help but chuckle as he yanks me up higher on the bed, and passionately presses his lips to mine. I know I'm forever his and that if he asked me to stay, I mean really asked me... I would.

The Climb

The airport's busy with people rushing to check in their luggage and return home. Meanwhile, my heart's breaking, knowing that in less than a few hours, my flight leaves and I must leave Phil, the only man I've ever loved. Sitting at a small coffee shop outside the gates, Phil and I remain fairly silent. The ten tables of customers come and go, with disposable cups full of caffeine, preparing for their flights. I pick at the scone on the plate in front of me and glance up to the man who's shown me so much in the past few weeks. A tear falls down my face, and he leans across the small, high-top table to wipe it from my cheek.

"Don't cry, baby girl. We'll be together again soon. I'll call you in three days when I get home. Your number's in my cell. Then we can begin to make arrangements for our next visit."

"I know. I guess I just don't want this to end."

"Neither do I. Here... let me write my number down for you, too. Maybe that will make you feel a little better. Do you have any paper?"

I dig through my purse, but can't find anything to use. I wish I had brought my cell with me. I pull an old receipt out of my wallet. "Here, use this. It's all I can find," I chuckle.

"That will work." He takes the scrap of paper and writes his cell and home numbers on it.

Placing it safely back in my wallet, the boarding announcement for my flight comes over the intercom and my heart sinks. He stands and offers me his hand, guiding me up to my gate. Looking up into his bright blue eyes, I notice them start to moisten and glisten in the light. Throwing my arms around him, I begin to sob, feeling like a teenager for doing so.

"Oh sweetie, don't leave me like this. I hate seeing you hurt."

With his index finger, he pulls my chin up to meet his lips. I'm swept away by the taste of him, as our lips move together. Swiping my tongue across his, he pulls me tighter to him and my need for him grows. Just seeing him takes my breath away, but being in his arms and feeling his touch numbs me. His hand runs up and down my back, trying to soothe and comfort me. Then a voice speaks out.

"Miss, you are our last passenger. We need your ticket."

One last hug and I turn to board the plane, handing the tall women in the navy blue suit my boarding pass. I pause for a moment before turning down the hall, Phil standing there with a weak smile as he waves and blows me a kiss. Everything in me wants to turn back and run into his arms, but I smile back and continue on my way, tears streaming down my face.

By, Charlotte Blackwell

Once the plane's in the air, the flight attendants walk around offering drinks and headphones. Pulling the headphones from my purse that I saved from my flight here, I order a drink in hopes of calming myself a little. Opening a mini bottle of vodka and pouring it into the small plastic cup, then filling it with soda, the flight attendant hands it to me. I pull a five out from my wallet to pay for my beverage, before settling back in my seat. Flying coach has really come a long way since the last trip I took. The larger seat is much more comfortable. I slam back my drink and instead of watching the in-flight movie, I decide to listen to some music. Leaning my seat back, I make myself comfortable and close my eyes. This is going to be a long flight; nearly thirty hours with transfers.

I don't really know if I completely zoned out, but before I know it, I'm walking off my connecting flight. My heart still aches, but at least I know I'll talk to Phil in a few days when he gets back to New York. Oh god, I didn't tell him... I never told him that I love him. That's the first thing I'm going to do when we talk. For now, I find myself looking around the air terminal and feel a sense of home. Hobbling to the baggage area, I see my mom and her jaw drops at the sight of my cast.

"Oh, Trista, what on earth happened to you? I knew going on this trip by yourself was a bad idea."

"Mom, calm down. I'm okay. I tripped on Kili and fractured my ankle. I met some great people there, and they took care of me."

"Why didn't you come home when this happened? I could've taken care of you."

"Mom, I love you, but I'm a grown woman and I can take care of myself. I made the decision to go on this trip and I wanted to see it through. This was the most amazing experience of my life. I've grown so much, and I even met someone." I smile at the thought of Phil.

Walking across the terminal hall, mom grabs one of the baggage carts and wheels it towards me. Pointing out my large red suitcase, my mom grabs it, placing it and my carry-on in the cart. I decide to push the cart for support, and Mom goes ahead to bring the car around. I just want to go home and sleep for a few days until Phil calls. I have two days before I have to return to the office; a job that I loathe. For now, I know I have to go to Mom and Dad's. The family will be waiting to hear all about my travels, and I miss them too.

The Climb

∞ ∞ ∞

Walking into Mom's house, the whole family's there to greet me. Dad's been working hard, making homemade burgers and fries. The house smells of deep-fried potatoes and reminds me of our weekly family dinners. I hear the sound of little footsteps echo down the hall, as my two nieces come running into my arms.

"Auntie!" they scream.

"How are my girls? Did you miss Auntie?" I ask while embracing them in my arms.

"Yeah... did you bring us anything?" Paige asks, with her big green eyes sparkling at me.

"Don't I always have a treat for my girls?"

Mom brings my bag and places it on the pale brown coffee table. Unzipping the bag, both girls are pinned to my side, excited about the gifts they will soon receive. Sharing stories about my trip and explaining about the climb up Kili where I fractured my ankle, everyone laughs knowing that an injury was to be expected with my two left feet. I pull out shirts from Tanzania for my parents, my nieces, my brother, and his wife. Giving T-shirts to commemorate a trip started with my brother, and carried on with my mom. Whenever they'd travel, those of us back home would receive a shirt, a tradition I can now continue. I pulled out two giraffes from my bag, one for each young girl. Explaining that in Africa they're called Twiga's, and sharing the story about kissing one at the giraffe farm shortly before falling from the jeep and suffering a concussion, again my family chuckles. A few more gifts from the various places Phil took me to see, and its dinner time.

My sister-in-law, Kate, starts the questioning. "So, who is this Phil guy you've mentioned several times now? And why do you light up every time you say his name?"

"Phil... what can I tell you about Phil?" I smile again, "He's the most amazing man I have ever met. Sorry, Dad and Will, you two are right up there, too."

"Yeah right, you were always looking to replace your big brother."

"Oh, shut up. Now Phil... well, he saved me on Kili. If it weren't for him, I would've never made it to the summit. After he insisted on helping to care for me, he still made sure I enjoyed my trip. He had the penthouse suite and insisted that I stay in the spare room, so he could keep an eye on me."

"Was he there with anyone else?" Mom wonders.

"No, here is what's amazing. His wife passed a year ago from brain cancer. Okay, well that part isn't amazing. It was her dream to climb Kilimanjaro, so he did it for her and placed her picture and a small vial of her ashes at the summit. It was one of the most emotional things I've ever seen. I was getting to know him as we climbed up the mountain, but to see with my own eyes, the exact moment he got closure on his wife's death, well, it is indescribable."

"That's a very touching story, my dear," Mom smiles.

After a few more stories, and once dinner is finished, I can't help but to excuse myself. I just want to get home and I'm grateful that my car's parked here. Enlisting my brother's help, I get my luggage loaded and he follows me home. It's nice to be back in my own car, with my music. I'm glad that I can still drive with my cast on and even happier that my condo has an elevator. I drive through the streets of San Francisco and see all the traditional buildings that make up this beautiful city. The Victorian architecture still takes my breath away; the grand arches and the greenery creeping up the walls and fences is second to none. I pull into my parking space and before getting out, I wonder what's going to happen next. Phil will be back in the U.S. in just a few days, and I have no idea what to expect. I fell in love with the most remarkable man, but we live on opposite ends of the country. Tonight, for the first time in weeks, I'll be going to bed with him nowhere near me.

I settle into my apartment and decide it's a good time to go through a few things. Opening my purse, I dig through my wallet to find Phil's number. I need to know that I have a way to reach him… to speak with him again. My heart begins to pound as I look frantically. Unable to find the paper with his number on it, I remember the drink on the plane; I gave the flight attendant a five-dollar bill, and the paper with his number must have fallen. How could I have been so careless? Fearful of never being able to talk to him, I throw myself on my bed and begin to sob. Still exhausted, I cry myself to sleep, drifting into a dream state where I can see Phil again.

Chapter 12

Phil

The past four days without Trista have been the longest of my life. Now that I'm finally back home in New York, I'll call her today as promised. I'm excited to hear her voice again and tell her how much I've missed being with her. We are going to have to figure out our relationship and the situation, something that will keep us close to one another. I wait as my driver pulls around to the pickup gate at JFK airport and helps load my luggage into the back of the black sedan. With the bumper-to-bumper traffic of the big apple, it takes nearly ninety minutes before we pull up in front of my Manhattan high rise. Excitement begins to rush through me, knowing that in a few short moments I'll hear her voice again. I only hope she hasn't had a change of heart. The time I spent with Trista in Africa holds more meaning to me than any other experience before.

Once we reach the penthouse, I pull out a fifty and tip my driver before he leaves. I look around the home I left several weeks ago, and although I feel comfort and a sense of relief being back home, I only wish that Trista could be here with me. I place my suitcase by the overstuffed brown leather sofa and walk through the open area around the large island to my chef's kitchen. I open the double-sided stainless-steel fridge for a soda. The fridge is fully stocked, just as I requested. As I crack open the can of cola, the fizz pops and sprays, making me smile at the memory of Trista having a soda explode on her in Africa. I can't wait any longer; it's time to call my girl. My heart skips a beat with the excitement of hearing her voice again.

Grabbing my cell phone and opening the French doors, I walk out to the balcony. The trees and the park surrounding my apartment building are a beautiful site. Africa has given me a new appreciation of my surroundings and nature. Placing my phone and soda on the patio railing, I pull a chair over and brush the dust off the cushion before sitting down. I can't understand why I'm so nervous. We have such a connection and fell in love, but what if she changed her mind, or it was just a fling for her? As I sit back in the chair and try to encourage myself to call her, I remember all the fun times we had. I reach forward to grab my phone, feeling the brick of the railing as I reach for it. My fingertips touch it, and as I move further, the phone begins to vibrate and topples to the ground, some thirty stories below.

With my heart sinking into my gut, I race to the elevator, pushing the button repeatedly in hopes it will arrive at my floor faster. It only takes moments to reach the main lobby, but it feels like ages. I'm hoping I can salvage Trista's number from my phone, but my gut knows it will be impossible. I scour the ground and find only bits and pieces on the road. As I continue to look for my SIM card, an older woman holding a large red purse begins to hit me with her bag, screaming at me.

"You idiot, if that would have hit someone, it could have killed them. I don't have many years left, but I sure don't want death by cell phone. You moron. Why would you throw your phone over the edge of a high rise?"

"It was an accident, I had my phone on the ledge and when it vibrated, it fell. I'm so sorry; I didn't mean to harm anyone," I frantically try to explain.

"Well next time, be a little more careful. You were lucky this time," she yells and smacks me with her bag one last time before continuing on her way.

Her words resonate through me. Lucky? Lucky? How am I lucky? I have no idea how to reach Trista now. Sadness runs through me at the thought, and then I think... Google! I have to Google her. I race back up to my apartment and turn on my desktop. Waiting for my computer to load, my heart races faster with every passing second.

I release a breath as my home page pops up, and quickly type in her name, "Trista Smith." Various pages pop up and I skim through such ones as Facebook and Twitter but don't see her. I type her name again, but this time, I add San Francisco to the search. Still, about five pages of results come up; I look at every page to no avail. With each click of the mouse, my heart sinks deeper. The thought that I may not be able to reach her tears at me. Trista brought such feelings of life and joy to me; something I wasn't sure I'd feel again after Sara's death. I only now realize that Trista could be my soul mate, the love I had for Sara was amazing, but Trista's different... special. I can't let her go, not like this. I continue searching the net for hours, trying to find anything that may lead me to her. The jet lag begins to set in and I can no longer search, as my eyes begin to close, and my head feels as if it were being crushed in a vice.

The Climb

Leaving the computer on, I stumble into my room and toss my clothes to the floor as I undress, and flop onto my huge, soft bed. Instantly asleep, I open my mind and invite Trista into my dreams as I drift further and further away. It's as if she's right next to me; I can smell the vanilla of her hair and skin. Holding my love close to me, we begin to kiss, our lips touching ever so softly as my tongue duels gently with hers. Pulling her closer to me and wrapping my arms around her small waist, I feel peace and comfort in her arms. In my dreams, her leg is healed, and we get a little frisky. Picking her up from the bed, her toned and sculpted legs wrap around my waist. In the throes of passion, I slam her back against the wall. Her moan rumbles between the two of us. As she slides her hands up the wall, I lift her teddy over her head. Her hands lower back down to me, caressing my chest with such love and admiration. "Oh god, Trista, I love you." Before long, we're back on the bed moving as one. Falling next to her on the bed, I take her in my arms and fall asleep. Trista continues to fill my dreams for the next eight hours.

By, Charlotte Blackwell

Chapter 13

Trista

I've been home for almost a month now and still, haven't heard from Phil. I don't want to believe that was the last time I'll ever be in his arms. I've searched everywhere online that I can think of, and can't even remember the name of his company. Maybe he doesn't want to talk to me; after all, he has my number in his cell phone. I guess I could always chalk it up to one hell of a fling, but it wasn't a fling for me. I've never had anything like that before, never shared anything like that with anyone. I try to put all thoughts about him behind me as I get ready for work. I need to move on. Men and I just don't mix; guess that's why I've always avoided relationships. I just can't believe I meant nothing to him, that it was all just a game for him. I don't want to lose him, but I think he's gone and I miss him with every fiber of my being. No matter how hard I fight it, thoughts of him consume me. I need to move on, I need to forget about him, but can I?

After a day filled with tons of meetings, Katie and I decide to go out for a drink after work. The little martini bar around the corner from my downtown office is the perfect place. We enjoy going there because it's not filled with all the punks that are finally legal. It has an age requirement of thirty, which means we don't feel like a couple of cougars out on the prowl. A lot of the office workers from the area frequent the quaint spot, since it's perfect to relax after a long day. After packing up our belongings, we walk to the bar. It's really only about twenty steps from our office building.

"Trista, we need to cheer you up. I know you were really hoping to see this Phil guy again, but I think it's time to move on."

"I know, Katie. I just really thought we had something. Typical man, out for a bootie call while on vacation. I bet the whole story about his dead wife was just his way of trapping some chick into feeling sorry for him. I'm such a fool."

"Na girl, we've all fallen for that crap before. Just remember the fun you had and then find someone else," she chuckles.

"He promised to make me feel like a queen, and I believed him. How stupid can I be?"

"Girl, you're being too hard on yourself. You're a beautiful woman and it's his loss."

"Well, let's see if I can find the last nice, available guy left in San Fran."

"I'm sure you will find more than one. You're a catch and a half." She nudges me while pulling open the door to the martini bar.

We enter and look around the elegant club for a table. The comfortable atmosphere is just what I need. It's dim in here, with small chandeliers barely aglow, dark walls, and checkered pattern flooring adding to the ambiance. The small, intimate tables and little leather chairs look more like a living room than a bar; they're so inviting. The bartender's pulling out all his moves for those that choose to sit on the bar stools. Mimicking Tom Cruise in that cult classic, 'Cocktail,' he flips bottles in every direction before pouring the liquor into the shaker. Girls are surrounding the bar, watching him work his magic. Katie and I notice an empty table near the back corner and snatch it up before the rest of the after-work crowd comes in.

A tall, thin waitress walks over. "Hey ladies, what can I get you tonight?"

"Two of your nightly specials, please," Katie replies.

The waitress smiles, nods, and turns to walk towards the bar. Every night, the bartender offers a different special drink, something he creates. Most of the time they're pretty good. Other nights, he could've stayed at home, because even I could do better. I'm hoping tonight it's one of his better concoctions.

A few moments later, the waitress walks over with our drinks and sets them in front of us. They're a pretty purple color and smell sweet. Katie and I lift our glasses, clink them together, and with our eyes locked on each other to gauge our reactions to the first sip, we both move towards the thin rim of the glass. The sweet liquid moves down my throat and warms me. After a few sips, a wave of warmth flushes over me. Placing the drink back down, I excuse myself and run to the restroom. Barely making it to the toilet, I begin throwing up.

"Trista, are you okay?" Katie walks into the restroom after me.

Wiping my mouth, I look up at my friend, "Not sure. I guess whatever that drink is, it doesn't agree with me." Suddenly, another wave hits and I bury my head in the toilet again.

"Okay kiddo, I think we need to get you home. God only knows what you could catch from sticking your head in that bowl."

Once my stomach settles, I agree, and Katie helps me home. I toss my keys on the small table near the door and head into my bedroom. I have a modest apartment; it's all I can afford. It's in a decent neighborhood, and it's comfortable enough for me. About eight hundred square feet of carpeted bliss. The large windows look out to the street and my bedroom's near the back. It's a perfect set up so that I don't get all the street noise when trying to relax. I really hate getting sick. I wonder how many days of work I'm gonna miss from whatever this bug is. I don't like the idea of being hung up in bed for any amount of time. When I'm by myself with nothing to do, that's when I think of Phil the most. I want to continue to search for him, look online some more to try to find him. I've tried every investment banking firm I can find in New York, searching their company directories for him, with no luck. I can't help but wonder if he's even an investment banker, or if that was just part of some made-up story to suck me in. I don't know what is real or fake with him anymore. I've been trying to keep myself busy, so I won't be overcome with thoughts of him. I tend to beat myself up for believing he cared. Then I start making excuses for him as to why he hasn't called. I still hope he does. Even though I've practiced giving him a piece of my mind, I'm sure I won't be able to resist him and I'd fall right back into his trap. Devastated, I remove the necklace he gave me and toss it on my nightstand.

By, Charlotte Blackwell

Chapter 14

Phil

I can't think of any other ways to try to contact Trista. Last week I took my cell phone pieces to the repair store, in hopes that they could extract the numbers from the memory – no such luck. Turns out I saved her number right to the phone and not the SIM card. My next plan of action is to contact my buddy, Mark. Mark's a private investigator, so maybe he can help. I can't lose her. After Sara passed, I never thought I'd ever find another love, not like that... but I did. There's no way the universe could be so cruel as to take two loves away from me, could it? Trista's the most beautiful woman I've ever seen. Sara was amazing and I'll always love her, but Trista is just as amazing, inside and out. Should I feel guilty about that?

When I return to work, she's still all I can I can think about. This makes it difficult to concentrate on my projects. I've delegated some of my work to my employees, but if this goes on much longer, I'm going to go crazy. As my mind continues to wander, the phone rings, snapping me out of my thoughts and bringing me back to reality.

"Good afternoon, Phil speaking."

"Hey, Phil. Mark here. Haven't seen you since you got back from Africa. I'm downstairs at the pub. Do you have time to come meet me?"

"Dude, were your ears ringing? I was just thinking about you. I have something I need to discuss with you."

"K... should I order you something or you gonna be a while?"

"I'm already packing up to leave, how 'bout a pitcher for the two of us and some deep-fried pickles?"

"Sounds perfect man, see ya soon."

The Climb

∞ ∞ ∞

Doc Watson's pub is busy today. Doesn't look like we'll get a chance at the pool tables tonight. Walking through the traditional Irish pub, I notice Mark in a small corner booth and make my way back to him. Mark sees me and begins to pour the amber ale into a frosted mug across from him. Sliding onto the red leather covered bench, I smile and shake my old friend's hand. "So glad to see you, Mark. How the hell have you been?"

"Sorry, it's been so long. I've been good, how about you?"

The last time I saw Mark was shortly after Sara's funeral. He's always been there for me, but I think I just shut everyone out and poured myself into my work. I can't let that happen again. I can't avoid everyone that I care about. Luckily, Mark and I've been friends since grade school and can go years without talking, but pick up without skipping a beat the next time we see one another.

"So, what's up, bro? You said you wanted to talk?" Mark douses his deep-fried pickle in ranch dressing and takes a bite.

"I need your professional services. I recently returned from vacation in Africa, and... well... I met someone there."

"You fucking dog, did you get your bang on?"

"It's not like that – I mean... yeah, I did, but it's more than that."

"So, she was good and you wanna get more?"

"Okay Mark, enough. You need to stop being such an ass!" I feel my blood start rising at the way he is talking about Trista. In the heat of the moment, I just shout, "I'm in love with her!"

"Oh, sorry man, I never thought... I just assumed you were starting to play the field a bit. So, you love her. Well, tell me more about her."

"You wouldn't believe me, but she's the most beautiful woman you could ever imagine. Her hair is long and silky smooth, and her eyes, oh my god, her eyes... they tell such a story. Then there's her personality, I mean she has a brain about her too. Anyway, I went to call her after returning from Africa, and my phone fell off my balcony and smashed. I can't find this girl anywhere. This is all I have on her." I slid a brown manila envelope across the round bar table. It contains a few pictures of us and any information I have on her. Her name, the city where she lives, her flight info from Africa, and the memory card from my phone that no one else could retrieve the info from. Any other information I could remember from our trip or what she told me is also included. I just hope it's enough.

"I'll see what I can come up with, bro. I can't promise, but I'm very good at my job."

"I know you are; that's why I brought this to you. I trust that you can find Trista for me."

Mark and I enjoy a few drinks together, and I tell him all about the adventures I had in Africa. He also shares a little bit about himself. Mark's actually seeing a girl. I guess the hound dog's finally getting trained. I must admit, I miss our time together and we both agree not to let it go so long before we see each other again.

Tonight, I decide to go visit Sara's headstone. Although some of her ashes are on top of Kilimanjaro now, her gravesite's a place I can go and feel close to her. I need to explain to her about Trista. I know she can hear me and has been watching over me, but I feel a little guilty falling for someone else. I'll always love Sara, but I need to move on too like she wanted me to.

Walking up to her gravesite in the beautiful cemetery, I marvel at the colorful rose bushes in whites, yellows, reds, and pinks. Various other flowers are in full bloom, as well. I notice her parents there. "Mr. and Mrs. Roberts, it's nice to see you again. Sorry I haven't come by to visit you."

"Phil, honey, it's wonderful to see you. We understand. You needed to deal with the loss of Sara on your own time. We knew we would see you eventually." Sara's mother wraps her arms around me.

"Phil, son, how are you doing? I heard you fulfilled our daughter's wishes and took her ashes to that mountain halfway around the world." Mr. Roberts places his large, strong hand on my shoulder.

"Yes sir, I just got back a few weeks ago. I should have spoken with you before I left; it's just been so hard to face the loss of her. I'm sure you both understand better than anyone."

"Yes, Phil, my wife and I do understand. That's why we haven't pushed the issue with you. I must say, you look as if you finally have closure. Why don't we sit down and you can tell us about your trip."

The three of us walk the ten steps towards the large white bench the Roberts family donated to the cemetery in Sara's name. It's a place we can come and be near her, remember her.

"Well, where do I begin? I planned on telling Sara all about my trip when I came here today, but I guess I can tell all of you. I spent quite a while there. Climbing Kili took nearly a week. I was with a great group of people and it was difficult, but the entire group made it to the top. One woman was injured on our last leg of the climb, but we made a stretcher and carried her to the top. We needed to rush down and get back to the base, where she could be rushed to the hospital."

"Wow, it sounds like a very exciting trip, and this young lady was very lucky." A soft smile crosses my former mother-in-law's face.

"Well, that's not it. This was the most amazing trip. I had a chance to say goodbye to Sara one last time, and close that chapter of pain and anguish of my life. Although, something I never expected, happened on my trip."

"I hope it's something good, Phil. Why don't you tell us more," Mrs. Roberts encourages.

"Of course... well, you know I loved Sara so much. I never expected to move on from the loss of her. She'll be with me forever. But... I met someone in Africa. She's amazing, and although she can't replace Sara, she has taken over my heart and mind." Taking a deep breath, I continue. "Her name's Trista, and she was one of the people on the climb with me. She was the one that got injured and I helped to care for her. During our time together, I fell in love with her. I feel a little guilty because I was on this trip for Sara."

"Son, stop right there. Mother and I understand. You can't stop your heart from loving. We are sad that Sara's gone, but we've accepted it, and you have to as well. We couldn't be happier that you have found someone to love again. Will we get the chance to meet her?"

"I sure hope so, but the thing is, I haven't been able to get a hold of her since I returned. She lives on the west coast and... well, to make a long story short, I lost her number and can't find her now."

We sit together for over an hour as I tell them all about Trista, and how I believe it was Sara that brought us together. They really seem happy for me. I have to find her; I can't just let her think I don't want her.

By, Charlotte Blackwell

Chapter 15

Trista

The past few weeks have been hell. I've resorted to keeping a separate garbage bin by my desk. Later today, I have an appointment with my doctor to go over some tests she ran. I hope it's nothing serious; maybe I caught a little something over in Africa. Getting through the day at work's been difficult, and my nights are spent curled up in bed. I want to look for Phil, but don't have the energy. I've finally realized he played me so well... and I just want to thank him... for reminding me why I'm still single. How could I possibly think that some guy I met on top of a mountain could be interested in me? I mean come on! The whole story about Sara was probably all part of his game. Nothing more than some trust fund jackass, traveling around the world, seeing how many chicks he can get in the sack. Oh my god, I hope I didn't catch some kind of STD from him. I'll find him and kill him.

I can't find Phil anywhere. I mean, who doesn't have Facebook these days? Is his name even Phil? Taking a deep breath, I mentally count to ten, trying to calm myself. *Face it, girl, you got played*, I think to myself for the hundredth time. What I don't understand is, why does my heart still yearn for him?

A few hours pass and I feel my phone vibrate on my hip. Looking down to check, I see a text from my mom. *I'm waiting downstairs for you, sweetie. Couldn't let you go through this alone.* Putting the phone back in my case, I grab my coat and let the receptionist know I'll be out for the rest of the day.

"Trista, will you sit down already?" Mom grabs my hand and tugs me toward the chair next to her.

"Mom, I can't sit. I can't anything. I wish you could understand how scared I am right now. Look at me. I've lost ten pounds already. What if it's cancer, or what if the fuck head gave me HIV? I'm too young to die!" Tears run down my face faster than I can wipe them away.

Mom grabs me and holds me as the medical assistant walks towards us. "Trista, let's get you in the room now."

Hand in hand, my mother and I follow the heavyset woman into the room. A single exam table sits in the center, with an armchair to the right and an office chair at the small desk with a computer. I hop on the table as my mom pulls the chair closer to sit next to me. Within moments, Dr. Lee enters. The short, thin, Asian doctor sits in the other chair.

"Hello, Trista. How have you been feeling since I last saw you?"

"Not any better. The nausea and vomiting isn't subsiding at all, and I'm losing weight faster than a tree loses leaves in the fall. I have to be honest... I'm so terrified right now."

"Oh, Trista what on earth are you so scared about?"

"What you called me in here for. Look, just give it to me straight, am I gonna die?"

"Die? My lord, girl, no! Honey, you're pregnant."

"I'm WHAT?"

"You're going to have a baby, my dear. I'd like to do a sonogram right now, so we can determine exactly how far along you are. Then we can discuss your prenatal care. Just lay back and I can do the exam."

Laying back on the exam table, mom stands next to me for support. As Dr. Lee approaches, I take a deep breath and she asks me to raise my shirt a little. She tucks a small, blue paper cloth into the top of my pants and squirts a blue gel on me. It's freezing cold, but Dr. Lee comforts me as she explains the procedure.

The monitor beside me begins making a swooshing sound. I begin to panic as the doctor explains. "That's your baby's heartbeat. Would you like to see?"

Looking at mom and back at Dr. Lee, I nod with nervous anticipation. She turns the screen towards me and points at a small little flicker on the screen.

"This little blip is your baby's heart. It's hard to make out the baby yet, but a few more weeks and you should be able to see every little detail. From my calculations, you are right around nine weeks."

"I kinda figured as much. I've only been with one person and that was in Africa, which was just over two months ago. We spent a few weeks together, so it doesn't leave much of a window."

"Oh, so the father isn't in the picture? Do you want me to go over other options for you?"

"Other options? No, I could never...I mean there's nothing wrong...I just... I'm capable of raising a child on my own."

"I hope you know I didn't mean to offend you."

"My daughter understands, Dr. Lee; I think she's just a little overwhelmed. Would you mind setting up the prenatal appointments and call me with the schedule? I think my daughter just needs to process all this."

"Of course. I'll have my receptionist call you tomorrow with the next appointment. Here is a prescription for Diclectin. It will help with the sickness and it's safe for the baby. Just follow the instructions the pharmacist gives you. Most of all, make sure you stay hydrated."

Mom decides to take me to her place. I don't say much on the way there. I'm pretty sure I'm in complete and utter shock. Just hours ago, I convinced myself that Phil's nothing more than a jerk and now, I'm carrying his baby. What the hell am I going to do?

Chapter 16

Phil

This has been the longest six months of my life. Every day since I returned from Africa, I've searched for the woman that captured my heart on top of that mountain. Just as I'm ready to give up on my search for Trista, my phone rings. I've since had my cell replaced, with the same number, just in case.

"Hello."

"Hey, there brother, how you been doing?"

"As good as I can I guess. How are you, Mark?"

"Not too bad. Sorry, I haven't reported back in a while, I was following a lead."

"Well, I wouldn't worry about it anymore. I think it's time to move on. I can't keep hoping for her to drop out of the sky and suddenly be found. Maybe she doesn't want to be found."

"Phil, stop right there. I think I found her! Trista Smith of San Francisco isn't the easiest task, but I got a girl that matches almost everything. I've booked us a flight for tomorrow. Can you make that work in your schedule?"

"Yeah, dude, of course, I can. How long?" The excitement of finding her is setting off every electron in my body.

"I got open-ended tickets, so we can stay as long as we need," he announces.

I begin to make arrangements for my departure. I'll work from my laptop as much as possible. I can't believe that I might finally see her again. I hope she still wants me as much as I want her.

By, Charlotte Blackwell

∞ ∞ ∞

It seems to take forever for morning to come and of course, I don't get much sleep. I have the town car arrive at the condo at seven and head over to Mark's place. Our flight's at eleven, so we have plenty of time. Neither of us says much as we sit in the airport lounge. We just both sip on a whiskey. I don't normally drink this early in the day, but something needs to calm my nerves. I still can't believe after six months, I'm about to see her again. Then panic begins to set in. What if she doesn't want to see me again and that's why she hasn't called? What if she's found someone else? Whatever it is, it doesn't matter. I have to see her. Worst-case scenario, I have to get closure. I just don't want to believe that she was only a fling. We had a connection and that's what I have to hold on to.

"Can I please have all business class passengers for Flight 132 to San Francisco precede to the boarding gate?" Says a timid, young voice over the intercom.

Mark stands and smiles, "Well bro, are you ready? Let's go find your girl."

With a nervous breath, I grab my carry on and nod. "Ready as I'll ever be. Let's get this show on the road."

We make our way to the boarding gate and through the tunnel to the plane. Once we sit in the overstuffed black leather seats, the rest of the passengers are allowed to board. Now I just can't wait to get there. I want to see Trista and let her know why I didn't contact her, that I didn't forget about her and how much I love her. This is going to be the longest six hours of my life. I just pray she hasn't found someone else and forgotten about me. I'm not me without her.

∞ ∞ ∞

Mark and I make our way to the rental car counter located in the airport, and grab an Eclipse Spider convertible in candy apple red.

"Damn, this is a nice fucking car, Mark. I may have to look into getting one for myself when we get back to New York," I say, as I walk around the outside of the car, checking every little detail.

"Ok brother, are you here for the car or to get your girl?" Mark smiles, jumping into the driver seat.

Jumping over the door, I plant myself in the passenger seat. "Let's go find my girl."

Putting the car into drive, Mark begins our mini tour around San Fran and towards our hotel.

By, Charlotte Blackwell

Chapter 17

Trista

I feel like a house. I can't believe how big my belly's getting. Only three months left to go until this amazing little miracle that Phil has given me arrives. I guess it wasn't all bad. He made me a mother and at least on my part, this little munchkin was made out of love.

"Trista, are you ready for your checkup?"

"Yeah, I'm ready. I can manage by myself now mom, you don't need to miss work for this. I can handle it on my own."

"I know you can, darling. Just remember... this is my grandbaby and I love being able to share this with you. I don't want you to feel alone, just because you're a single mother. We are here for you, even if you can't get a hold of this Phil character. I didn't get to experience as much with your brother's kids, so now it's my turn. Sorry about your luck, but you're stuck with me enjoying this."

"Mom, you can't be upset with Phil. He might not be around, and who knows if what he told me was the truth, but he's made me a mother... something I never thought would happen."

"You're right, sweetie, but we better get going or you will miss your checkup."

Mom and I both get in the car. My doctor's office is only about twenty minutes from my apartment, but it's right downtown, so traffic can be a little unpredictable.

"Are you getting excited? You're in your third trimester now and it's coming up fast. I think after your appointment, we should go shopping for the nursery. What do you think? Mom's treat!"

"Mom, you are amazing. I only hope I can be half the mother you are."

"You will be Trista, don't you ever worry about that."

The Climb

We continue on our way, chatting about what we need to get for the baby. The roads are busy for midafternoon. In my rearview mirror, I notice the nicest convertible behind me. It's cherry red and smoking hot. Two men sit in the front seat. I can't help but think the guy in the passenger seat looks a little like Phil. This pregnancy brain must be playing tricks on me.

"TRISTA, WATCH OUT!" my mom screams.

I look at her and she's pointing out my window. Before I can react, a semi-truck plows through the intersection and sends us spinning. Everything goes black and all I hear are horns and screams echoing through the air, followed by screeching tires. Not understanding what's happening, I try to move, but can't. I can't see anything. I only hear the sounds around me. Why can't I feel anything? I should be in pain. Oh my god, where's mom? Is mom okay? The baby... what about my baby? Panic starts to set in, but I have no idea what's happening. Now all I can hear are footsteps running towards me before I drift off and lose it all.

By, Charlotte Blackwell

Chapter 18

Phil

Driving through downtown San Francisco I can't believe how beautiful it is…right up until the small car in front of us gets t-boned by a semi-truck. The compact car spins 360 degrees and slams into a lamppost. The driver's side is completely crushed. I can't help but assume the driver is dead.

As Mark slams on the breaks, I toss him my phone and shout, "CALL 911 NOW!" and I jump out of the car to race to the aid of the victims.

Approaching the passenger side of the car, I can see two women. I'm able to pull open the door. The passenger's lucid, but has a large gash on her head, which is pouring blood. Tearing material from my shirt, I hold it to her head. "Don't worry ma'am, help is on the way."

"My daughter, she's…she's expecting. How is she? How is Trista?" The weak and weary voice begins to crack.

My heart starts pounding from my chest at the sound of her name. Spinning my head to look at the other victim, I realize even through the mangled metal, it's my Trista. The woman said she was expecting. She found someone else. My heart sinks. That doesn't matter right now. I have to save her. "Hold this to your head and I'll check your daughter."

As she takes the torn piece of my shirt, I race to the other side, reaching through the broken glass to check for a pulse. "Ma'am don't move until the medics get here, but your daughter has a pulse. It's weak but she's still alive. I'm gonna hold her head to make sure her neck is stable."

Mark runs to the woman and helps her. I can hear the sirens in the background; I know they're getting close. I hold Trista's head still between my hands and notice the blood pouring from her abdomen. I fear for her baby. If I know Trista at all, and I believe I do, this will destroy her. She seems to be unconscious, so I decide to release her head and put pressure on her abdominal wound.

The Climb

"Mark, how's your patient doing?"

"Not bad, brother, but I don't want to move her. How's yours?"

"Still breathing, and I still have a pulse, but she's hurt, man. This is her, this is Trista." The tears begin to fall down my face as I hold another woman that I love in my arms to die. This can't be happening, not again. Am I cursed? I wonder.

I hear the emergency crews pull up and as a medic taps me on the shoulder, I share a little report about Trista and the history I know.

"Thank you for your help, we have it from here," the forty-something man with graying black hair says.

"I'm not leaving her. She's the love of my life."

"Okay son, go to the rig and you can come to the hospital with your wife." Then he turns back, so he and his partner can care for her. Placing a cervical collar on her, they look for a way to extract her from the car.

The second unit takes care of Trista's mother, once they secure her and remove her from the car. As they wheel her to the ambulance, I reassure her that I'll take care of Trista and that I won't leave her alone.

I sit by the ambulance as instructed by the medic, and watch as the fire department comes in with the *jaws of life*. Trista's trapped in the twisted metal and they need to cut her out if they're going to try to save her. The creaking and ripping of the metal sends chills down my spine and the police officer has to restrain me from running to Trista's aid. I can't bear to think of the pain she must be feeling. I can't lose her... not like this. I can handle that she's found someone new, but I can't handle her not being here anymore. The medics carefully pull her from the torn metal, placing her on a backboard and strapping her down. I move further in the ambulance as they race over with the stretcher. Once she's in the ambulance, they flip the siren on and a firefighter slams the rear doors shut. I hear a bang on the back door, signaling the driver they are cleared to leave.

Trista's being connected to all kinds of machines and an IV is started. I sit in silence as the primary care medic yells reports to the driver, who then reports back to the hospital.

"Sorry to bother you, but will you be taking her to the same facility as her mother, the other passenger?"

"Yes sir, we will be. It should only be a few moments, but she'll be going directly into surgery to deliver the baby."

"It's too soon, you can't take her baby."

"From my measurements, she's around twenty-eight weeks, does that sound about right?"

"Wait... twenty-eight weeks? That's a little more than six months!" I slowly panic as the realization hits me.

"Yeah, six months. Does that sound right? When did you find out you were having a baby?"

I take a deep breath, thinking to myself 'about five seconds ago.' I need to let them believe we're together, or they won't give me any more information. "Yeah, that's right. She conceived when we were in Africa."

"Okay sir, I don't want you to panic. I know this is all terrifying, but at twenty-eight weeks, your baby has a very good chance of surviving. He or she will be in the NICU for a while, but assuming no serious damage was done from the accident, it should be fine. Let's just get her to the hospital and let the doctors take care of your family for you. Once the baby's delivered, they can treat your wife and child for any injuries."

"Umm… yeah… but she's not my… we're not married… yet, but you have to save her, so I can make her my wife." I bury my head in my hands. My baby. Trista's been dealing with this all alone. Is that why she never called? Because she didn't want to scare me away or trap me? Maybe she doesn't think I'm father material. MY BABY! We have to save them; I need to save my family.

∞ ∞ ∞

I can't just sit here and wait; it's driving me nuts. After all this time, I've finally found Trista and now I find out I'm going to be a father. The doctors have taken her into surgery. The gash to Trista's abdomen is deep, and the medical team is concerned that it might compromise the baby. I don't know much about this kind of stuff, but I'm not sure if a baby can be born this early, despite what the medic told me. Mark followed us to the hospital, but I sent him on his way and promised to keep him updated.

As I pace the hall with concern, a nurse approaches. "Are they okay? What's going on?"

"Sorry sir, I have no information about Trista or the baby. Although her mother's now awake. I can take you there."

"Thank you, I'd like that."

I follow her down the hall into a small room. An older version of Trista sits before me.

"Phil, I assume? Please have a seat. I think you and I need to have a little chat about my daughter."

"Yes, Ma'am."

"The nurse has already told me that Trista and the baby are in surgery. I assume you had no idea about Trista being pregnant?"

"No, Ma'am. I haven't seen or talked to Trista since she left Africa."

"And why is that, young man? Even more important, why are you here now?"

"I tried to call her, but broke my phone and lost her number. I had hoped she'd call me, but she never did. I hired a private investigator to find her. That's why I'm here. I couldn't just let her slip away from me. And now I finally found her... and she is having MY baby... and I may lose them both," I cry, almost unable to control my emotions as I look at the life I could have.

"Phil, we are not going to lose either of them. Now you go wait for some news on them and report back to me as soon as you find anything out." She smiles weakly and rests her head back on the pillow, obviously tired.

"Ma'am, are you alright?"

"Okay, first off stop calling me Ma'am; my name's Katherine. I'll be alright, just a little sore... and the medication's kicking in. Thank you for asking. Now go check on our girl."

By, Charlotte Blackwell

Chapter 19

Trista

Help, someone, please help my baby. What's happening? Why won't you look at me? I continue to run the hallways, asking everyone for help, wondering why they won't answer me, look at me, or help me. The blood and pain from my abdomen is terrifying me. I don't know what to do. How did I even get here?

I sit in the chair and try to compose my thoughts. Ok, I'm at the hospital... but how did I get here and why won't anyone help me? Where's my mom? Is she okay? Then I notice Phil run past.

Phil? Phil, what the hell are you doing here?

He doesn't respond, so I decide to follow him. This has got to be some kind of bad dream. With footsteps thumping behind me, I stop to check the commotion and then it all becomes clear as a nurse runs right through me. I must be dead. But why am I still feeling pain? I begin to think to myself, 'Trista, get it together. Go find out what happened.' I shake myself out of it and run after Phil and the nurse.

Down the long, white hall and through a set of double doors, I see Phil pacing in front of another set of doors. I make the call to go through the second set of doors and pass right through them. I find myself in an operating room; a large white room with a huge, steel light, and numerous medical staff members surrounding the table. Peering through, I see myself and my heart sinks. As the room spins around me, I hear the beeping of the heart monitor; I'm alive... I'm still alive.

"Neo team, are you ready? We have a baby girl, about twenty-six weeks in my estimation. Get ready to bag her, I don't have any respirations," says a man working over me. Then he turns, holding the tiniest little baby I've ever seen. She has no color; her skin's translucent.

The Climb

The nurse I followed grabs her, taking her to a smaller table where a team begins to work on her. Oh, my baby... my baby girl. Falling to my knees, I begin to pray. *Oh lord, please save my little girl. Today's the first day of her life, and her daddy's right outside. Let her be okay. I know it's not time for her to be here yet, but she is. Please, let her have a chance to live, to love, and to enjoy this beautiful world you have given us. Take me. I've had my chance. Let her live and take me to be your angel.*

Rising from my knees, I watch as four nurses and two doctors work on my little miracle girl. One is using only a finger to do chest compressions, while another is connecting a breathing machine.

"Nurse, administer the surfactant. This baby's in infant respiratory distress. Her lungs aren't developed enough," a young doctor orders.

"Yes, Doctor. Everything else is ready. The cardiac-respiratory machine can be started," she responds, as she pushes a vial of surfactant down the breathing tube.

"Ok, we have a pulse and respiration! Let's get this little peanut warm."

As the team continues to work on her, I hear the doctor behind me announce that my injuries are stable and the incision is closed.

"Let's get the baby to the NICU. Does anyone know if the family is waiting?"

"Yes, Doctor. Mom's mother is admitted as a patient, and baby's dad is just outside the OR."

"Thank you. I'll go report to him on both mom and baby's conditions. Admit mom to ICU. I want her monitored closely... her spleen took some blunt trauma and I want to make sure I don't have to go back in for it."

"Baby's stable, weight is 900 grams. This is going to be a long haul, but we've pulled it off before," announces the other doctor.

I follow the surgeon that worked on me to the hallway. I want to make sure Phil's going to be here for our baby. How did he even know?

By, Charlotte Blackwell

Chapter 20

Phil

hy is this taking so long? They've been in there for over an hour. I just want to know what's going on.

"Excuse me, are you Dad?" a man in green scrubs asks.

"Yes sir, my name's Phil. How is Trista and our baby?"

"Let's have a seat and I'll explain." He points to the chairs against the wall. As we both sit, he begins. "My name is Dr. Manning. I worked on Trista and delivered your daughter. They're both stable right now."

I let a tight breath escape from my lungs. "Thank God. Thank you, Dr…"

"Don't thank me yet. This is not going to be easy. Your daughter's very little, one of the smallest we've ever delivered here. She's only 900 grams and about twelve or so weeks early. The mortality rate for preemies born this early is high. Her lungs aren't mature enough for her to breathe on her own, and we have to use a heart-lung machine. There's a lot we need to discuss, but I want to give you time to process all of this. You will need to decide if you want us to use all available efforts to save her. We will meet later with the entire team to go over your daughter's care and treatment. For now, do you have any questions?"

"Um, yeah, I mean, I… I don't know. I… uh… have a daughter? What about Trista? How is she? I… I don't know what to do." I throw my head down into my hands.

"Trista endured some injuries, and she will be recovering in the ICU. I hope for her to wake in the next hour or so. You can see her once she's assigned to a room. Would you like me to introduce you to your baby?"

"I don't know. I mean I should wait for Trista. I want to see her, but it just doesn't feel right. Can I maybe just see her through a window?"

"There's no window in the NICU… the neonatal intensive care unit is not a happy place. We have very ill newborn babies there and don't want the general public viewing it. I really think it would be good for you and the baby if you to come meet your daughter."

I get a sense of peace, like he is right... like Trista would want me to go and be with our little girl. "Yes, I think you're right. I'd love to meet her."

"Follow me. Once we get there, you will need to dress in scrubs and I'll also teach you how to scrub up. We're very protective of these babies and everyone that enters needs to wash thoroughly. We can't take the chance of bringing illness in. Now, you are currently healthy, and have not been in contact with any chicken pox or other communicable diseases, right?"

"No, I'm fine, and no one around me has been ill."

We continue to walk and take the elevator to the third floor. Passing the regular nursery, I look at all the happy families and healthy babies, unable to even wonder what our little girl will look like.

"I want to prepare you... your daughter's very, very small and although anatomically, she is normal, she doesn't look like these other babies. She has no fat and her skin is very thin. Remember, she hasn't fully developed yet. She's also going to be hooked up to machines and in a warmer."

"I'm ready Dr. Manning."

Inside the nursery, I'm introduced to the staff and they explain how to prepare myself before going in to see the baby. I must check in with them, wash my hands and arms up to my elbows for at least two minutes, but five is preferred. Then I have to put on a yellow gown over my clothing. Once that's all done, I go over a small checklist to ensure I'm healthy and won't bring any illness into the NICU.

"Okay, Phil, let's go meet your daughter," Dr. Manning smiles.

We walk past the washing area and nursing station. The following area is filled with babies of various sizes, ages, and health. So far, it's not looking so bad. Some of these babies are small - really small - but so far, I just see heart monitors and oxygen tubes. Some of the babies even look healthy and normal, so to speak.

As we turn the corner, I see what looks like a mini suntan machine. The little one under the lights has these little foam sunglasses covering his eyes. The doctor explains it's a treatment for jaundice and that preemie babies commonly get it, but in most cases, it's very treatable. The further back in the nursery we walk, the more I see, and panic begins to take over. What do they do... hide the worst cases in the back?

"Here we are, Phil. This is your little girl." The doctor stops in front of this small, enclosed plastic case-type thing. It has two little holes on the side, with small doors and rubber sleeves inside.

Inside is a tiny little alien-like creature, with a large tube attached to her mouth and tons of wires everywhere. She has no eyelashes and her skin is so thin, I can see the purple from all her veins. My heart begins to sink. How can this be our little girl? What kind of life is she going to have? Placing my hands on the incubator, I rest my head on top and looking down at her, I begin to cry for the sweetest, most beautiful little alien-girl in the world. Right here, right now, I'm looking at my very own heart. She's my life, my love, my world.

Chapter 21

Trista

Why did I follow them in here? My God, she is so small and fragile. It looks like she's smaller than Phil's hand. Why can't I just wake up? She needs me... he needs me. What a shock this must all be for him. He didn't even know I was pregnant, and now this. *Phil, I need you now, and our daughter needs you until I can wake up.*

As I watch him sitting next to our baby girl, I can't help but wonder how long he's gonna be around. Things were so amazing in Africa; I really thought he loved me, and then nothing. Now he's back. I just don't understand any of this. I wanted to kill him for having sex with me and then ignoring me when we returned to the States. I mean really, who the hell is that rude. I really have to stop worrying about that right now. My main concern should be our baby and waking up, so I can care for her. God, I have so many thoughts and feelings right now.

Okay, time to find myself and wake up! I walk through the halls of the hospital and make my way to the ICU. There I find myself, or at least my shell, my body. I don't have all the machines that my baby has, but there are enough. Within moments, a nurse and doctor walk in. They do a quick check of my vitals and begin to discuss my condition.

"I don't understand. She should have woken up by now. I see no signs of brain damage."

"You know how it goes sometimes, Doctor. When a patient goes through such a trauma, their bodies just shut down until they are ready to deal. We have to assume that's what is happening here."

"Yes, but I would still like a CT, just to make sure there is nothing underlying. Has her family been in to see her yet?"

"No, her mother's admitted here as a patient, and the baby's father is in the NICU with their daughter. Would you like to speak with them?"

"No, that's fine. I'd prefer to have more answers for them. Let's try and get this young woman to wake up."

Shortly after they leave the room, a porter comes and takes my body to diagnostic imaging. I follow close behind, hoping I can learn something about my condition, and how to wake up. My daughter needs me... and I need answers from Phil.

∞ ∞ ∞

I don't really have a sense of time, but according to the clock, it's been several hours and the doctors still don't seem to have any answers. A nurse brings my mom in to see me. She looks so fragile and torn. She needs me too, so why can't I just wake up? I wish Dad was here. Why does he have to be out of town at a time like this?

"Trista, baby, come back to us. Your little girl needs you... I need you. Phil came back for you. He lost your number just like you did his. What are the odds? He loves you baby, and he's been looking for you this whole time." Mom begins to cry at my bedside.

Mom, I love you. I'm right here, and I'll come back to you all. Just make sure my baby is okay. I need your help until I wake up. I wish she could hear me.

Chapter 22

Phil

It's been a week since I found Trista and discovered we were having... well... *had* a baby. Trista still hasn't woken up, and the doctors say the longer she doesn't, the less her chances are of *ever* waking up. I refuse to settle for that. I will not lose another woman I love. I will not lose the mother of my baby. Today I'm insisting on trying something new. Our baby has been somewhat stable and I've heard other parents talk about kangaroo care; where you take the premature baby and cuddle, skin to skin. Apparently, the warmth and the sound of the heart helps the baby improve. I'm hoping this can work both ways. On my demand, the doctors have agreed to move Trista to the NICU, so we can take the baby from the incubator and do kangaroo care with my two girls. They'll both be closely monitored to ensure no drastic changes in vitals or movements that can harm either of them. The doctors have explained that they normally don't do kangaroo care with micro-preemies, but are willing to try, for Trista's sake. I have to believe that holding our baby will help bring Trista back to us.

"Mr. McKay, are you ready for us to transport Trista now?" the nurse asks politely.

"Yes, she needs to hold our daughter. Do you hear that baby? You're going to meet our little angel."

The nurse and a porter transfer Trista to a movable bed that's much smaller and easier to maneuver than the typical hospital room bed. I follow them as they push her toward the nursery. Because Trista's unable to scrub, the nurse does it for her. I scrub up and put on the thin yellow gown and mask as well. I'm excited for her to meet our daughter, and for our baby to meet her mama.

"Ok, sir, we're ready to take her to the parent room."

They move Trista into a separate room at the back of the nursery. It has a bed, a chair, a washroom, and glass doors. The nurse and porter transfer Trista to the bed in the room and connect her to the monitors. Once they're done, a NICU nurse brings in our baby and connects her to another set of monitors. She gently open's Trista's gown, exposing her chest. She then removes the baby from the incubator and strips her to only a tiny little diaper. She places the baby on Trista's chest and covers my two beautiful girls with a warm blanket.

"Mr. McKay, will you please sit next to them, to ensure the baby's safety?"

"Yes, of course." I sit on the bed next to the two people I hope will be in my life forever and begin to get a little choked up. They're a beautiful sight. Trista and I made this little angel out of our love for one another, and now, here we are... together.

Glancing up at the heart monitors, I notice both of their rates equaling out. Their oxygen saturation is between 99 and 100%.

The nurse stands in amazement as she calls to the doctor, "Doctor, you won't believe this. Little baby Smith-McKay, her oxygen, and respirations have never been this stable. We only just placed her in kangaroo care. I have never seen it work like this."

"Looks like mom's vitals are stabilizing too. Sir, do you mind if we document this on video for training?"

"I don't mind. I assume this is good?" Then I feel something warm brush against my hand. Looking down I see Trista's hand move over the baby. She moved! This is the first time she has moved.

The doctor calls security and informs them that all footage from this room is to be saved. Apparently, they have running footage that records on a loop until notified otherwise, in case of an incident. Other doctors, including Trista's neurologist, begin to file into the small room to witness the miracle before us. I knew this would work... I knew holding our baby would help Trista.

"Sir, I'd like to try mom without oxygen, and I'd also like to see if your baby can breathe on her own without the respirator. It's unlikely she will stay off it this soon, but I'd like to see what happens."

"Is it safe?"

"The risks are minimal. I just feel that with the way they are both improving together, it's worth trying. I don't want to rush things, but the fewer machines either of them are on, the better."

"Alright, let's give it a try."

"Nurse, please have the CODE team standing by, I don't want any delays if things go a different way."

The doctor slowly walks towards the small baby wrapped in Trista's near lifeless arms. Once he has the baby in arms reach, I move out of the way. As he disconnects the tube connecting the machine to the tube in her throat, I watch with bated breath. They gently remove the intubation tube from her throat. The nurses and doctors have moved in close, and I can barely see either of my girls through the medical team. Everyone watches in silence until we hear a cough. Not a baby cough, but a soft, raspy adult cough. I push my way through and watch in disbelief as Trista opens her eyes.

"Oh my GOD, it worked! I knew it would work! I told you. Trista, baby I'm here." I push through to get closer to my girls and kiss Trista on the forehead as I sit next to them.

The medical staff begins whispering about the baby, "Look, she's doing it, she's breathing on her own. I can't believe this. Today, we are witnessing a miracle."

"Trista, do you hear that, baby? Our daughter's breathing on her own. This is our girl, our baby, in your arms." Unable to control my emotions, the tears run down my face.

By, Charlotte Blackwell

Chapter 23

Trista

What the hell just happened? Where am I? I mean, I know I'm in the hospital, but just a few moments ago, I was watching everything from the sidelines, and now it's all blurry. How'd I wake up? God, I just want to go back to sleep. This is so overwhelming. Phil... he really is here. That was one hell of a dream I had. Wait... I have a baby in my arms. She's so small. Oh my god, she's mine! How long have I been out for? Is she going to be okay?

I begin looking at the mass of people in the room, but I only recognize Phil. His hair's everywhere and it looks like he hasn't shaved in a while, but he's still just as adorable. Wait... why's he here? Oh my god, I don't think I can handle this.

"Trista, baby, it's okay. You were in a car accident. I found you after months of searching. Our baby had to be delivered early and you've been unconscious for several days... well, over a week now. Your mom's okay and you will be too. Don't panic. It will all make sense in time, my love," Phil says, in an attempt to calm me.

I'm so confused. I haven't heard from him in months and now he's here, acting as if we are a couple. "What the hell is going on?" I manage to squeak out, my throat sore and dry.

"It's a long story, but I broke my phone, lost your number and have been searching ever since. The PI I hired thought he found you, so we came to see if he was right. When we were driving from the airport, there was a car accident. We stopped to help and that's when I discovered it was you. I've been by your side ever since, and I've even gotten to know your mom. I never wanted to be apart from you and I'm so sorry it took me so long to find you."

He really expects me to believe that BS story? Whatever... I don't even know what to believe right now. I need to figure out what's going on with my baby. I just look with disbelief, since it's too hard to talk. I realize I don't remember anything from the past week.

A tall, slender man steps forward. "I may be able to help you understand, Miss Smith. My name is Dr. Manning, and I'm on the team that has been caring for your little girl. She's what we call a micro-preemie. She has been doing very well, but today we thought... correction, Mr. McKay thought something called kangaroo care might benefit both of you. This is why we have you and the baby in skin-to-skin contact. He was right; we've seen an improvement in both of your vital signs since we started kangaroo care. Now that you're awake, I'd like to put the baby back into the incubator and examine you. We can also explain everything that's been happening over the past few days."

"Thank you, Doctor, that sounds good," my raspy voice whispers, filled with confusion and questions.

My thoughts are so jumbled; I don't know what's real or a dream. I remember seeing Phil here in the hospital, but how's that possible if I've been unconscious for over a week? I haven't seen him since Africa. Seeing him stand before me with such concern just makes me melt, even if I want to hit him for not contacting me for six months. I'm not sure what I'm going to do, but I hated missing him. This doesn't make it easy for me to forget him. Is he really coming back to me?

He touches my hand. "Trista, I know you must be overwhelmed, but I'm here and I'm not leaving. It will all make sense, in time. All I ask is that you don't turn your back on me. We can get through this together. I've never stopped loving you and now that I've found you, I can't let you go."

"Mr. McKay, I'm going to have to ask you to step out for a few minutes, so we can examine Miss Smith. May I suggest you go tell her mother the good news?" Dr. Manning encourages.

"Yes Doctor, her mother will be very excited and I'm sure she'll want to come see her," Phil says, as he kisses my hand and leaves the room.

"Miss Smith, may I speak freely with you?" the doctor asks.

After a sip of water, my throat begins to clear a little, "Please do, Doctor. I'm so confused. Is my baby going to be alright?"

"Oh yes, she's doing very well. She still has a long road ahead of her, but every day she survives, her chances of a long-life increase. I'd like to offer my opinion on Mr. McKay. I realize it may be a tad unorthodox and I apologize if I overstep. I've never seen anyone so concerned before. I could tell he wasn't aware that you were expecting, but he has accepted that little girl wholeheartedly. He only leaves to shower and eat; he has stayed by your side every night. When your baby was born, he wanted to wait for you to meet her, but I convinced him to bond with her. A baby and parent create a special bond, and it's so important when they are so small. All I'm suggesting is that you give him a chance to prove to you that whatever happened was a mistake or an accident."

"Thank you, Doctor. I appreciate your honesty. I don't know what to think or believe right now," I say, with tears streaming down my face.

Dr. Manning smiles. "It's okay to feel that way. A lot has changed for you in the past week. Why don't we go on with the medical exam, and then I'll let your mother come see you. And if you'd like, we can get physical therapy up here to begin working with you. The sooner we get you moving the faster you will heal."

Wiping the tears from my face, I smile and give the doctor a small nod.

Chapter 24

Phil

With a sense of relief, I walk down the halls of the hospital to Katherine's room. She's going to be so excited that the kangaroo care worked, and Trista's finally back with us. I hope that one day she'll forgive me for not contacting her. I'd have had my numbers backed up. After I speak with her mom, I need to go to the gift shop and get Trista something. Better yet, I'll go now and bring her mom some flowers to celebrate the good news.

Heading back up to Katherine's room, my arms are full with a large arrangement of flowers, a pink blanket for the baby, and a gift bag full of things for Trista, including a small bear that says, 'I LOVE YOU'. As I reach Katherine's door, I notice she's sitting in a chair eating her lunch.

"Good afternoon, Katherine. How are you doing today?"

A warm smile greets me. "Feeling much better, thank you. The doctor's releasing me today. How are you, and how are our girls?"

"Well, that's why I'm here. I brought you some flowers..."

"Flowers? What the hell happened? Do you really think flowers will make it better?" She begins to sob.

Placing the items down, I walk over to the woman I hope will one day become my mother-in-law. "Katherine, you didn't let me finish. Everything's okay... better than okay. I brought you flowers to celebrate. We placed the baby in Trista's arms, and she started breathing on her own. Then Trista woke up. They are doing amazing."

As she sucks back the tears, she says, "Oh Phil, I'm so sorry I jumped to conclusions. I couldn't be happier. How is Trista doing?"

"She's pretty confused and scared. I figured you'd want to go see her."

"Of course! She must be freaking out. Will you take me now?" she asks with excitement.

"The doctor was just examining her when I left, but I'm sure by the time we get there they'll be done. Do you need a wheelchair?" I ask.

"Do I look like I need a wheelchair? I'll race you there, punk," she responds with a giggle.

We walk to the elevator and take it to the NICU on the third floor. After we both scrub up and sign in, we go to the room Trista and the baby were in earlier. Trista's sitting on the edge of the bed with a nurse by her side, and the baby is in the incubator next to her.

"It's nice to see you up. I brought back a surprise for you," I announce while entering.

"MOM!" Trista screams and reaches out her arms. The two women embrace, and tears flow down both their faces.

Katherine pulls back and looks Trista in the eyes. "Sweetie, I'm okay. How are you feeling?"

"I'm okay, Mom... a little weak and scared, but okay. Can you believe I have a little girl? She's so small."

"Yes, she is. She's our little peanut. If she is anything like you were as a child, she will prove to be a fighter and she'll be fine."

"Phil, thank you for bringing my mom to me and thank you for being here. The doctor told me you haven't left and I can't thank you enough for your support."

I walk over and sit next to the ladies on the bed. "There's nowhere else I would rather be than with my girls... all three of you. I'm sorry I wasn't here sooner. I'm just grateful I found you when I did. Talk about fate."

"Okay Phil, we need to get one thing straight. There will be no more apologizing. One day in the near future, we can discuss what happened, but from what I gather, we both just had some bad luck. None of that matters right now. You're here now, and we can begin to work on what we need to do about our daughter. First order of business... I think she needs a name; baby Smith-McKay isn't much of an identity."

With a small grin across my face, I nod. "What were you planning on naming her?"

"I hadn't thought about it much, but now that you're here and considering how we met... well, it was Sara that brought you to Africa, so what do you think about Sara Tanzania McKay?"

I begin to tear up, unable control myself. After everything, she still wants to honor my deceased wife and me. With a deep breath, I suck back the salty tears. "I think that's beautiful, but are you sure you want to name our daughter after my late wife?"

"I know how much Sara meant to you. I also believe that if it wasn't for her, we would've never met and this beautiful little baby wouldn't be here. If it's too much for you, we can think of a different name."

Placing my hand on hers, I respond. "I think Sara is perfect. Thank you so much for the amazing honor. Am I being presumptuous to assume by giving her my last name that you will allow me to be a part of her life?"

"You're already are a part of her life; I hope that we can work on you being a part of mine as well." Trista smiles softly, and I fall in love all over again.

By, Charlotte Blackwell

Chapter 27

Trista

When the doctor was talking with me, I finally remembered everything from the last week. I realized everything I saw was like an out of body experience. I guess I was witnessing everything going on around me, which made accepting Phil back into my life easy. I hope that one day we can become a family. I've never loved before and don't think I could ever love anyone the way I love Phil. Our love grew fast and deep. I don't foresee it being difficult to pick up where we left off.

Together with my mom and the father of my beautiful little girl, I feel blessed. A car accident, a coma, and an emergency delivery, and yet we're all here and doing well. Anything else can work itself out later.

Phil whispers softly, "I love you, Trista, and I'm so happy I finally found you."

Turning to him, I kiss him softly, and memories of our brief but passionate time in Africa flood through me. Finally - able to tell him for the first time, I say, "I love you too, Phil."

Everything seems perfect; the pieces of our lives falling into place like a puzzle. Then Sara's alarms start blaring and my heart sinks. The doctor rushes back in, and a full team of medical personnel follows.

"What's going on, what's happening to my baby girl?" I scream.

A nurse comes and escorts my mom and Phil out of the small room, explaining the need for room to work on Sara. I can feel the pain Phil's going through, as I'm just as scared for our little girl. We can't lose her... not yet... not now; I just met her and love her more than anything.

With the doctors and nurses surrounding Sara, I can't tell what's going on. I can hear beeping and see them rustling around her incubator. Before long, the beeping stops, and Dr. Manning comes to sit next to me. The nurses take Sara and her incubator out of the room, allowing Phil and my mom to rejoin us.

"I realize that must have scared you, but Sara's okay," the doctor reassures. "The nurses have taken her so they can restart her IV, get her body temperature back up, and monitor her closer to ensure the ventilator doesn't have to be restarted. The alarms you heard were caused by bradycardia, which is a decrease in heart rate for longer than ten seconds. We had to make sure her heart rate was stable. It also appears her temperature has dropped slightly. The nurses have adjusted the incubator to help warm her. During all our fussing, her IV got bumped, and because of how fragile she is, it needs to be restarted. I don't want you to be alarmed, but the IV will most likely be started in her scalp. This is one of the easier places to maintain a site on these little babies. It will be covered with a little plastic medicine cup to protect it. Do you have any questions?"

I look at Mom and Phil, still in shock, trying to understand everything that's going on. With tears in my eyes, I shoot Phil a pleading look. He takes my hand and smiles supportively.

"Doctor, is this set back because we tried kangaroo care?" Phil questions.

"No, I strongly believe that she benefited from the skin to skin contact, and I'd like to do it daily. We witnessed a true miracle today. This is just one of the things that happens with preemies. Think about it like this; the baby's connected to a heart monitor at all times. This monitor is going to pick up every beat or skip of a beat the baby has. We don't know if we, as adults, have intervals where our heart rate decreases because we aren't monitored twenty-four - seven. It's more of a concern if the heart rate changes for an extended period of time, or if it happens frequently."

"Okay, so what other kinds of things can we expect for Sara?" I question.

"Unfortunately, when a baby is born before its gestation's complete, they face many complications. Some include immature lung development, pneumonia, irregular heart patterns, jaundice, the inability to maintain body heat, immature digestive system, anemia, and many more. I don't want to overwhelm you with what could happen. Now, Sara has already experienced some of these conditions, and she may very well experience more, or possibly none at all. That's why it's best for us to focus on what is happening now. Sara's doing very well for her gestational age, and each day she survives, her prognosis improves. We aren't out of the woods yet, and chances are she'll need to stay here until her due date," Dr. Manning explains.

"Her due date? That's almost three months away! Sara's going to be in here for another three months?" I begin to cry.

"It's really for the best. We can monitor her here, and you can rest and heal at home. You're welcome here anytime, as there are no limits on visiting hours for parents. We encourage you to come as often as possible, Trista. You can even book the in-care room and stay the night."

Phil takes my hand. "Trista, Sara will be well taken care of here. Once you are discharged, we can start to get things ready for her. We can make plans and arrangements. We can come here every day and see her. It will all be okay."

How can he say it'll be okay? He lives across the country; I'm here with a baby that is going to be hospitalized for months. God, I don't even know how I'm going to afford all the medical expenses. Phil talks like it's our problem, but he'll go back to New York soon, and then what? Call every now and then? Maybe come and visit? I know what he said, but I just can't fully trust him yet. I don't want to get my heart broken again. My insecurities take over once again.

"What's wrong, beautiful?" he asks.

"I'm just trying to process everything. Like Sara's life, you being a part of it, medical bills, us, just... everything."

"Sweetie, I don't want you to worry about anything. I've already taken care of Katherine's, Sara's, and your medical expenses. I went down last week and gave them my banking information, so it'd all be dealt with and no one would have to worry about it."

"You did what? Are you serious? Don't get me wrong, I really appreciate the help with the financials, but I do have some insurance, and I don't want all the burden to be on you."

"Trista, I've worked very hard to make sure I was financially stable. Sara is my daughter, too. And you being her mother, and Katherine her grandmother, that makes you all my family, and I want to take care of my family. What is the point of having money if you can't take care of the ones you love?"

"Thank you, Phil, it means a lot," I respond, sucking up my pride, but still wondering if he'll be around for the long haul.

"As for everything else, it will work out. I want to be a part of Sara's life; I thought I made that clear earlier. I've already been making arrangements to transfer my office out here. My realtor's found a great office space and I've spoken to my lawyer; my business is going to expand. I'll have a New York office and a San Francisco office. My boss has been ready to retire for a while now, and I've agreed to buy the business from him. I have the right to do as I please. The staff's more than capable, and I'll promote someone in New York to run things from that end. I will also be able to create jobs here with the new location. It's all going to work out. I promise. Even if things between us don't work out, we still have our daughter to think about, and I want to be here... for both of you."

My mouth must be touching the floor; I'm in absolute shock. I know he said we'd work it out, but I had no idea he would just pick up and move here. My mom just smiles and nods at me. I know she thinks this is great. How did I get so lucky?

Chapter 28

Phil

It's been just over two weeks since I found Trista, and since our daughter was born. Today I have to leave them and return to New York. I need to make all the final arrangements for my relocation. I don't want to leave, but I have to. I need to instruct the movers about what I want to take from my penthouse and office. I need to sign the agreement for subletting, make some official promotions, and sign all the paperwork to take over the company. Wow, I hope I can get it all done in a week. I don't want to be gone for much longer than that, as the doctors think Trista will be released from the hospital around then. I want to be here when she gets out. Mark went back after only a few days, once his job for me was done. I was glad to have a friend around when everything went down. I'll have to meet with him, thank him again and make final payment for the services he provided. Christ, maybe I should make a list. As I run through everything that needs to be done, I notice Trista waking.

"Good morning, beautiful. Did you have a good sleep?" I smile at the woman that made me a daddy.

"Yeah, actually really good. Did you stay all night again?"

"Where else would I be?"

"Phil, you need to take care of yourself as well. You should go to the hotel and get some rest."

"Don't worry about me, this chair folds out to a little bed. I like being here for you and Sara. Although, I have to go back to New York today and finalize everything. I'll only be gone for a week at the most. I'm sorry that I'm leaving you, but I've left all my contact numbers with your mom, the nurse, and in your bedside drawer."

"I figured you'd have to leave at some point. You really don't have to do all this. Your life's in New York and I..."

"No! Stop right there! My life *was* in New York. You and Sara are my life and you are both here. So, this is where I belong... this will be my home."

Trista begins to cry, and I move to sit next to her and hold her in my arms. "Baby, it's ok, I don't have to go." I try to comfort her.

"No, it's...it's not that. You said you belong here because we are here. Do you really mean that? I mean... I never wanted to trap you, so when I didn't hear from you and then found out I was pregnant, I just assumed I'd be raising our baby alone. I never expected you to come back, so I convinced myself that everything in Africa was nothing more than a lie, a trick to get me into bed. Now that you found me, you are willing to change your entire life for us. It's more than I ever expected." She sucks in a breath and wipes the tears from her face.

"I don't ever want you to think you are alone in this. We're a team. Trista, baby, I love you... and I have ever since Africa. I never gave up looking for you. I want to be with you, and be with our baby. You are my love, my life, and hopefully, one day, my wife." I kiss her on the forehead.

"Your wife?"

"Yes, my wife. Not right this moment. I want to spoil you for a while. And one day, I'll surprise you, and I hope you will say yes...when the time is right, that is."

"Wow, I...I...don't know what to say," she stammers.

"Don't say anything." I smile. "Not yet, anyway."

"Well, I guess I better say good-bye. You need to go take care of some business back home."

"Not back home, back in New York. I already told you, *this* is my home now, but yes, I do. Will you be okay for about a week?"

"Yeah, I will. Oh, and Phil, I love you... I never stopped loving you." She smiles.

"I love you too, baby. I'll call you tonight." I kiss her and head over to the NICU to say my good-byes to baby Sara. This is going to be one long week.

∞ ∞ ∞

Back in New York, I don't even know where to start. It might as well be the office; get business outta the way first. Ben, my boss, meets me there, as do our lawyers. It only takes an hour to finalize the paperwork to make the company officially mine. Ben will remain on here, in New York, as a freelance consultant.

Together, we make the announcement to the staff and call Jake up with us. He looks terrified; I can't wait to see his expression when he finds out he is the new head of the New York City offices.

Ben takes the lead, "Good afternoon everyone. First off, I'd like to thank you all for your hard work and dedication. The past thirty years running this company have been the best of my life, but it's time for me to spoil the wife and travel the world. So, I'm retiring, at least for the most part. I've sold the company to Phil and he has some exciting changes he'd like to share with you. So, without further ado, your new boss and my successor, please give a warm welcome to one of your own, Phil McKay."

"Thank you, Ben. With new ownership, there are always some changes, but I want to assure you, these will all be good changes. I was trained directly by Ben, and things will still run the same. We do have two major modifications; first off, I'd like you all to help me in congratulating Jake Canmore, whom I'm naming as the new CEO of our New York offices."

Everyone cheers and Jake just stands there with a stunned look on his face. He's looking from me to Ben, to the staff, and back to me again. I pat him on the shoulder and ask, "So what do you say, Jake? Do you accept?"

Jake shakes his head, looking dumbfounded. "Ummm, yes sir, of course, I do."

"Great to hear! I have contracts in my office we can go over when we're done here. Okay! So now Jake will be running everything here. And where will I be, you may ask? Well, part two of our exciting news is that we are opening a branch office in San Francisco. I'll be heading up that office. We are expanding, and we'll be hiring new staff for that location. Of course, if any of you would be interested in joining me in relocating, please talk to Jake or myself and we can make the arrangements. Now, this is all exciting, but the most incredible news I have to share, and the reason for our expansion is... I've become a proud new father! The woman in my life delivered our baby a few weeks ago. That's why I've been absent the past few weeks. While out west, I secured the new location for our offices and I'll be fully transitioned out there as of next week. It's been a pleasure getting to know each of you, and this will surely continue. Our offices will be working hand in hand, continuing to provide the best investments for our clients. We will have staff seminars, retreats, and Skype meetings. I'm putting my trust in all of you because this is *our* company." I bow my head to the nearly fifty staff members that have worked with me for the past ten years here. I'll miss the friendships, but know it won't end when I get on the plane again.

As the others mingle and discuss the recent announcements, Jake joins me in my office.

"Well, congratulations Jake. How do you feel about all this?" I ask

"Pretty shocked, Sir, but thank you for having the confidence in me. CEO... my wife is going to be over the moon."

"Just wait till she finds out what your new salary is," I smirk.

"I didn't even think about that! I get a raise?"

"Of course, you do! What do you think would be fair?" I chuckle.

"Well, there is definitely more responsibility, and I guess I will need extra for entertaining clients. I make about $150k a year now, and I don't want to sound greedy, but would twenty-five percent be fair, Sir?"

"Twenty-five percent? You think twenty-five percent is fair?"

"Ummmm, I'm sorry... I really will be happy with just the title and the experience."

"Jake, stop! I think you better take a seat."

"I'm sorry, Sir. I didn't..." he rambles, afraid of how he thinks he offended me.

"Jake, seriously. You think you are only worth a little over $200k, doing the job of CEO? First off, you'll get a spending allowance. Here's a platinum Amex card for all work-related dinners, expenses, trips and such. You need to submit all receipts to Sonya, your executive assistant. You also get a new car allowance of one hundred thousand a year. I don't want you driving a mini-van. It has to be nice and represent our company. Then you'll receive a salary of seven hundred and fifty thousand a year, plus bonuses."

Jake literally passes out before my eyes. Jumping to his side I lightly slap his face, "Jake, Jake, wake up. You okay man?"

"What? What?" He stutters. "Did you say three-quarters of a million dollars a year?"

"Plus bonuses! Last year, I made a few million in bonuses alone. Now, of course, it will take time for you to make the kind of money I do, but with some hard work you will easily be making several million a year."

"Excuse me, Sir, but... are you fucking kidding me right now?"

"Jake, this is a stressful and strenuous job. You'll earn every penny of your pay. I'm not kidding; you are about to become a very rich man if you are up for the task."

"It has always been my dream, I just had no idea."

"Well, now you do, so let's get this contract signed, go get your wife and go car shopping. Then take your wife out for dinner. Oh, and tell her about your new position with the company and boom...business expense on the Amex card."

"Thank you, Sir. I won't let you down."

Chapter 29

Trista

I'm actually glad that Phil left for New York. Now I can begin to process everything that's happened in the past few weeks. Like the fact that he really does love me and searched high and low for me. Then, of course, the fact that it was him that saved my life, my mom's life, and our baby. Where do I even begin to start processing all this? Taking a deep breath in, I smile, knowing that I didn't lose him; Phil's going to be here with me and wants to marry me one day. We have a beautiful baby girl and I'm so happy. I always wanted a love like this and now I have it. I believe we'll be able to pick up right where we left off in Africa.

"Trista, sorry to interrupt, but the NICU just called and Sara is ready for her feeding. They thought you might like to come and do it," the nurse announces.

"I'd love to, thank you." I get up and move to the wheelchair she brought in.

As the nurse wheels me to the nursery, I can't help but feel blessed; like I'm the luckiest woman around. Once we get there, I do the required scrub and my nurse helps me put on the nursery gown.

"Hi, Trista. Someone has been waiting for you." The NICU nurse smiles and takes over pushing the wheelchair from my nurse.

"I'm excited to learn how to feed her properly. Thank you for calling me down."

We get to Sara's incubator, and I can see one of the other nurses checking her vitals and preparing her for her feeding.

"Hi Trista, are you ready for this?"

"I am, please show me what to do." I rise from the wheelchair and walk over to them.

The nurse shows me how they mix my breast milk with formula and oil to increase the fat content and thicken it slightly, so it's easier for Sara. They explain that preemie babies are susceptible to acid reflux. The thickened milk is easier for them to swallow. Today's the first day we're trying bottle feeding. Until today, she was tube fed. Apparently, we have to be careful. They explain that she can also develop oral aversion, which is something that can affect a child their whole life. There's so much to remember with babies, and when they are born too early, like Sara, there's even more.

"Okay, Trista, why don't you take a seat. Let's try to feed Sara while in Kangaroo care. She seems to respond very well to it."

I remove my shirt and they place Sara in my arms next to my chest. This is the best feeling in the world; holding my baby next to me, skin to skin, heart to heart. The nurse hands me the little two-ounce bottle that we prepared only moments ago. I've never seen a bottle so small. Taking it in my hand, the nurse instructs me to tickle Sara's lips with it and allow her to take the nipple, without forcing her. I do just as instructed, and Sara opens wide, taking the nipple in and almost instantly sucking. I can't help but smile. "She's doing it! Do you see this? She's drinking the bottle!"

"This is great, Trista. We really didn't expect her to suck yet. She's a little miracle baby," the nurse exclaims with sheer elation.

My little Sara *has* proven to be a little miracle. She's still super tiny, but defying so many odds and thriving. She's even started to gain weight. I'm so happy, and now I truly believe she'll be okay. I wish Phil were here to see this. He'd be proud of her. I'll have to tell him all about her feeding when he calls tonight.

Phil's only been gone for a few days and already, I miss him like mad. I thought I'd gotten over him, but having him here proved me wrong. I didn't want to melt right back into his arms... I just can't help it. I belong with him and I lose all control over my head when he's around because my heart takes over. He's part of me, and as much as I tried to fight it, I can't.

After Sara finishes eating, the nurse teaches me how to change her and we put her back in the incubator. She's getting some testing done shortly since we notice that she has a slight yellow tinge to her skin and they suspect she may have jaundice. From what I'm told, it's common in premature babies and easily treated. A simple blood test will let us know; I try not to concern myself with little things that Sara will most likely go through. The possible conditions she may encounter along the way is what scares me. The doctors have informed us of such things as brain bleeds, NEC - which is where the bowel dies, and something called ROP, which could lead to blindness. Those are the things that truly terrify me. I guess it's just best to take things as they come and not worry about what *may* happen. We need to stay positive for Sara and believe that she will live a long and healthy life.

It will be nice to get released from here, so I can start preparing Sara's nursery. With her being born so early, I didn't have the chance to get ready, so I only have a few items for her. I wonder how things are going to work with Phil and I; is he going to want to have her overnight at his place? Speaking of his place, I wonder where his place going to be?

"Trista... hello... are you still with us?" Mom walks in mocking me.

"Yeah Mom, sorry. Just daydreaming, I guess."

"What's wrong kiddo? Sara's doing great, and you've healed nicely from the accident and surgery."

"I know, it's just... what happens next? Where do I even begin?"

"Begin with what? With Phil? Honey, he loves you more than anyone has ever loved another person. That's the kind of love most people dream of."

"Trust me, Mom, I know. How did I ever get so lucky to find a love like this? I'm wondering more about what's going to happen once I get released, and especially when Sara gets released. Do we just start dating? I mean it seems kind of funny to start dating a man you already have a child with."

"Don't concern yourself with all the trivial things. Everything will work out the way it should. Your father and I are here to help you. Phil will be back in a few days and then the two of you can sit down and work out any details. Just be happy things are going good, my dear."

"Thanks, Mom. I suppose I just need you there to kick my ass every so often."

"What are mothers for?" She leans down and hugs me.

By, Charlotte Blackwell

Chapter 30

Phil

Almost everything is settled here in New York. I just need to go say goodbye to Mom and Dad and visit Sara's parents and her gravesite. It's both difficult and wonderful, closing this chapter of my life. When I lost Sara eighteen months ago, I thought my life was over. Never in a million years did I think I'd find another amazing woman, or have a beautiful daughter with her. I feel like the luckiest man in the world. The movers are just finishing up with the last of my belongings and my new tenant is already here. The inspection went perfectly and he's ready to move in. As I take one last look around, I decide not to draw things out any longer and take my leave.

I arrive at Mom and Dad's, they've invited Sara's parents over for lunch. I guess I can kill two birds with one stone. My stomach starts turning and flipping in every direction. How do I tell my wife's parents that I have a baby with another woman? I know they were happy for me when I told them about Trista, but this is a whole new ballgame.

"Phil, my boy, come sit and tell us what's new," Mr. Roberts insists.

"Good to see you. I'm glad you're all here together. Actually, I have some huge news."

"Did you find your girl? Oh, what was her name again?" my mother asks.

"Yes mom, I did. I found Trista. That's where I've been the past few weeks. Actually, when I found her, she was in a bad accident and I almost lost her. She's doing much better now and should be released next week," I begin to explain.

"That's wonderful! I'm glad she's doing well. Will you be going back to see her soon?" Mom asks.

"Well, that's the thing, Mom. I'm actually relocating to San Francisco to be with her. I leave later today."

The next few hours are spent telling everyone about the changes ahead. They're all so supportive. Now, I just need to get the nerve to tell them about baby Sara. *Okay, you can do this Phil. They are going to be so excited.* I take a deep breath in and out.

"There's more I have to tell you guys. See, when Trista and I were in Africa, it turns out she conceived."

"We're going to be grandparents?" my mom yells, and they all smile from ear to ear with excitement.

"Well, see... when she got in the car accident, the doctors had to deliver the baby. We have a baby girl. She's small, but a real fighter."

"Please tell us you have pictures," Mrs. Roberts asks.

"I do! She was born weighing only nine hundred grams, so she's very small. She grows stronger every day though. She's such a strong little girl." I pull out my iPhone and flip through the pictures of my two girls.

"Oh, Phil, they're both just lovely. Does your daughter have a name yet?" Mrs. Roberts asks.

"Well, yes...umm... we named her Sara Tanzania MacKay. We both feel it was Sara that brought us together, so Trista thought it was the perfect way to honor her. I hope you don't mind."

With tears streaming down her face, she cried, "Why on earth would we mind, Son? That's such an honor. The fact that Trista respects the love you and Sara shared is amazing. So many women would be jealous of a past wife, especially one that was so tragically lost."

"Phil, we can't wait to meet her, to meet both of them." Dad boasts.

"Well, I'd love all four of you to come out and meet them. Let me get settled and get Trista settled once she is released from the hospital, and then we can make arrangements for you to come out to the west coast."

Everyone agrees, and I feel a sense of relief. My flight leaves in just four hours, so I have to go say a final goodbye to Sara and check in at the airport. I say my farewells at the house and head to the cemetery.

As I approach her tombstone, I can't contain my emotions. "Sara, baby, I was so blessed to have you in my life and would've died a happy man, knowing that I'd found my soulmate when I found you. Losing you was the worst day of my life and I wasn't sure I'd get through it. But you never left me, did you? You were by my side this entire time; making sure I got through the pain and found love again. I never believed that one man could have two soulmates, but you have proven me wrong. Because of you, I have Trista, and now baby Sara. She has your strength and determination. I see that already. What did I ever do to deserve the love of not one, but three amazing women? Thank you for everything, Sara. I'll love you forever. Goodbye, my sweet lady."

By, Charlotte Blackwell

Chapter 31

Trista

Phil and Mom should be here anytime. I can't believe it's been over three weeks since Sara was born and since Phil came back into my life. Now, it's time for me to go home and get some sense of normalcy back. Although, I don't know how things can be normal when Sara is still here, and may very well be for months to come. Thankfully, I only live about fifteen minutes from here.

"Trista, we have some paperwork to go over with you," the nurse announces. "First and foremost, you must remember that your incision is still healing. The doctor has written a prescription for painkillers, should you need them. No lifting anything over 10 pounds for another three weeks, and no strenuous exercise, including intercourse. Although your staples have been removed, you're still healing internally. You'll also need to book an appointment with your OB-GYN for a checkup in three weeks. Do you have any questions?"

"No, thank you, I think I've got it. No lifting, no sex... not that we have to worry about that any time soon. Oh my god... did I just say that out loud? I'm so sorry." I shake my head with embarrassment.

"Don't even worry about it. I bet it'd surprise you how many new moms say the exact same thing," she chuckles.

I sign the papers and head down to the NICU one last time before I go home.

The Climb

"Good morning, beautiful baby girl. How was your night?" I say, leaning down to my little peanut.

Her nurse walks over. "She had a great night, Mom. I actually just weighed her and she is up again; almost three whole pounds now! Trista, she really's amazing all of us. I've never seen a baby advance as well as Sara. I must say, she has an angel watching over her."

"She's gained about two pounds in three weeks... is that even normal? As for the angel watching over her, that she does. I can't even explain how happy her progress is making me. Each day I can picture her life and what it will be like, once she is released. It gives me hope."

"Babies this small can gain weight quickly, just as they do in the womb. You should have hope; hope can get us through anything."

Just as I wipe a tear from my cheek, Mom and Phil walk in. I have a sense of peace, knowing he's back, and back for good this time. I don't know how I made it through life without Phil, without love, without the other half of me.

"Now there's the two most beautiful women in the world. Man, have I missed you both," Phil says, with such a sparkle in his eyes. Then he leans over and kisses me, and out of nowhere, the fireworks I felt in Africa shoot through me with lightening force. "Are you ready to break out of here?"

Looking down at Sara, I begin to cry, "I am, but I just don't know how I'm going to leave her here. The past three weeks I've been just an elevator ride away. Now I'm going home and she's not. I'm not sure if I can leave her...what if something happens?" Panic takes over, and breathing gets harder.

Phil guides me to the chair. "Sweetie, it's going to be okay, I promise. We're in this together and we can handle anything thrown at us. Why don't we get you home and we can come back later today? Let's just start small."

We spend a little more time with Sara before leaving. Phil takes my belongings down to the car, and I make sure the NICU staff has all our contact information. My heart sinks, knowing I'm leaving my baby girl, but like Phil said, we can start small and come back shortly.

"Okay beautiful, the car's out front. Sara, baby, Mommy, and Daddy will be back soon. You behave for the nurses, okay?" He smiles and reaches his hand under the little lamps they have Sara under to cure her jaundice. "Do you think we can keep her first pair of sunglasses?" he jokes.

"We save all the little things from our babies. We take her footprints every week, measurement sheets, sunglasses, and more. We've even started her baby book for you. Every milestone, we document for you," the nurse announces.

"This is truly an amazing unit. You all care so much; I don't know if parents like us could get through it without such wonderful staff. Thank you," Phil says, with sincere appreciation.

"It's our pleasure, Phil. Working on a unit like this takes a special kind of nurse, and we all love what we do. Some days are harder than others, but when we send a baby home and get pictures every year on their birthday... well, let's just say that far outweighs the bad."

∞ ∞ ∞

"Where are we going, Phil? This isn't the way to my condo," I say, as we drive down a road nowhere near my place.

"Well, I thought you might like to see the house I bought. Is that okay?" He smirks.

"You bought a house?"

"Of course, I did. I need a place to live and something big enough to raise a family. Your mom helped me pick it out." Turning and winking at my mom, his smile grows. "Here we are."

As we pull into a long, circular drive, I can't help myself and shout out, "YOU DIDN'T!"

"I did." He grabs my hand, "When I was looking for a place, your mom told me this was your dream house since you were a child. So, I approached the owner and made an offer he couldn't refuse."

"You bought the manor I've always dreamt of. That's a little presumptuous, isn't it?"

"I'd like to call it wishful thinking." He squeezes my hand. "Come on, don't you want to check it out?"

"Of course, I do, but you couldn't possibly have possession yet."

"Of course, I can! Money talks, baby, and I paid for all the moving expenses for the previous owner. He jumped at my offer and it's all ready for us... I hope."

Helping me out of the car, Phil walks with his hand in mine, up the cobblestone path to the large oak door of the house he bought for us. Handing me the key, he says, "Welcome home, my love."

"Phil, this is too much. You really shouldn't have. We still have so much to learn about one another."

"True, but just think how much faster we can learn it if we live together. Trista, sweetheart, I love you and I already lost six months with you. I don't want to lose any more time. Although, I've had the guest house set up for myself, just so you don't feel pressured."

"Phil, really..."

"Kiddo, just open the door. You're not going to win this one," Mom interjects.

I do as I'm told. Pushing the key into the lock, I take a deep breath and open the door. I've always wondered what it looked like on the inside. The outside is perfect; a large, two-story, brick and mortar house with a wraparound porch. The perfectly groomed bushes also wrap around the house, just beneath the porch, and there's large trees in the yard. In the center of the driveway, a flower garden, and water feature. The water pours over various rocks, into a pond filled with Koi fish. I used to drive past here and dream of kids running around the yard, playing and laughing, while I sit on the porch sipping lemonade. With the door open, I take a step inside and I'm blown away. The foyer is beautiful, with beige marble flooring and large, white, roman pillars on either side of the staircase, and the biggest crystal chandelier I've ever seen.

"So, what do you think, Trista? So far so good?"

By, Charlotte Blackwell

Chapter 32

Phil

really hope she's happy with the house; I love it. When her mom showed it to me, I knew it'd be perfect for us. "So, what do you think, Trista?"

"I...I...I think this is way too extravagant. Don't get me wrong, I think it's beautiful... more so than I ever imagined. I just can't even conceive of what a place like this cost. Besides, it's huge! Even if I *do* agree to move in here, don't you think it's a bit big for the three of us?"

"First of all, you don't need to worry about the cost. I've told you before, I want to take care of you and spoil you. Now I have two ladies to spoil, and I want both my girls to have everything they want. And not to sound like an east coast snob, but I've become accustomed to a certain way of life, and I intend to keep those standards. Besides, do you know how affordable housing is out here compared to New York? This place would have cost ten times as much back east."

"Haha, fair enough then; so why don't you show me the rest of this palace?"

Trista, her mom, and I go through each room of the house, one by one. Starting in the family room, we explore the large, open area with a stone fireplace that stretches the entire length of the wall. Her eyes are so wide as she examines every detail of the room. The large bay window faces the front of the house, with a direct view of the garden. I had some cream-colored leather furniture brought in; she sits in the overstuffed chair and lets out a sigh.

After a few minutes, we tour the rest of the house. There's a huge chef's kitchen, formal dining room, entertainment room, office, six bathrooms and five bedrooms between the two floors. There's no basement, but there's a small, private wine cellar. What Trista doesn't know yet is that the wine was made here. We have a vineyard out back, and a winery on the property as well. The guest house is commonly used for staff, but who knows what will happen. I have to ensure Trista is comfortable before making any decisions.

There are two final rooms to show her; the master bedroom is huge and covered in warm colors. The walls are a soft green, and the four-poster, king size bed is covered in a white duvet, embossed in green to match. Two large armoires and a nightstand on either side of the bed are adorned with antique lamps. The walk-in closet is fitted with shoe racks, jewelry drawers and more. The master bath has a double sink, separated by a make-up area. There's a footed bathtub in the center, and a large, double shower surrounded by glass. I had the bathroom painted light yellow similar to a bees body; they say brighter colors help lighten a mood. I want it to be a relaxing for her... peaceful.

"Phil, this is amazing. How did you know exactly how to decorate it?"

"Your mom kinda helped me with that. She also allowed me to take a peek at your condo, so I was able to get a feel for what you might like. Does this mean you approve?"

"More than approve, I feel like it's all a dream or a fairytale or something."

"I still have one last room to show you... Sara's room." I smile, as I lead her across the hall.

As she opens the door, the first thing we see is a beautiful mural painted on the wall. It was painted from a picture we took at the giraffe farm. Another wall is painted from a shot of God's window, where we took the helicopter ride and picnic. It showcases the bright blue sky, perfect white clouds, and the lush greenery of the ground. A circular white crib with a canopy sits in the center of the room, and a changing table sits against the wall. A small bookshelf with classic children stories and a few African themed stuffed animals sits in the corner. A rocking chair is nearby, so Trista can read our peanut to sleep. I've had everything Sara might need stocked; diapers, clothes, undershirts, and sleepers. You name it, I got it. She also has her own bathroom that I've filled with bath toys, shampoos, lotions and such.

"Oh my god Phil, you've thought of everything. I can't believe these paintings. They're amazing... just as I remember Africa. Oh, and this little-stuffed twiga...thank you, Phil. Thank you for everything." She starts to cry.

"Trista, don't cry honey. Phil did all this for you and Sara," Katherine says, as she hugs her daughter.

"I know Mom, but who does this? Who lives like this? I just can't believe how lucky I am."

"Baby girl, you deserve it all and more. Phil recognizes that, and he wants to be the one to give it to you. Let him; love him and enjoy your life."

"Your mom's right, Trista. I want to give you and Sara the world. This is just the beginning if you'll allow me."

By, Charlotte Blackwell

She turns to me and throws her arms around my neck, deep sobs coming from her as I pull her close. My heart aches for everything I put her through. I can't wait to start my life with Trista and our daughter; to make every one of their dreams come true.

Chapter 33

Trista

hil walked my mom to her car so that I could have a few moments to process everything, look around on my own, and just take it all in. What did I ever do to deserve this, to deserve Phil? I can't help but ask myself, why me?

Laying down on the plush king bed, I close my eyes and imagine the day that Phil makes me his wife, the day when Sara comes home, and we can live here in this amazing house as a family. Maybe one day we can even have more kids. In the background, I hear the front door shutting and footsteps coming up the stairs towards the room. I stay on the bed, still with my thoughts, wondering what will happen next.

As Phil walks in the room, I can smell his cologne and breathe in the amazing scent. Before I know it, he's crawling up the bed towards me. Feeling him near me is setting off electric currents throughout my body. I want him more than ever. Suddenly, the nurse's order of 'no sex for three weeks' rings through my head. I can't resist him, though. His kisses run up my arm, to my neck and a little bite to my ear before he presses his lips to mine.

It's as if we never spent any time apart; our lips move together in perfect synchronicity, as our tongues wrestle one another. Such passion, such heat; makes me want him even more.

"Trista, baby, I've missed you. I've missed holding you in my arms, kissing those tender lips. Most of all, I've missed being near you, with you. Please take me back baby, give us another chance."

"Phil, I thought we already agreed to try. I told you how I felt before you went back to New York."

"I know, I just have to make sure. I want you to want me the way I want and need you."

"I do Phil, more than you know."

"Have dinner with me tonight? Let's go visit Sara and then we can go for a nice night out on the town. No, scratch that; you are still healing from surgery. Let's go see Sara and then come back here for a romantic dinner and a movie. We can cuddle on the sofa just like our first night together in Africa."

"That sounds perfect. Thank you for everything, Phil. I can't begin to explain what it means to me."

∞ ∞ ∞

Tonight has been perfect, visiting our beautiful little peanut together and then coming back to this magnificent house Phil bought for us. I didn't realize before, but there's a full staff here and he had the chef prepare us a wonderful meal; grilled chicken in a white wine reduction, paired with a lovely green salad and some grilled root vegetables. I've never tasted anything so perfect before. Now we can just sit and talk, catch up on all that's been happening, and work out some details. Mom had packed an overnight bag for me, assuming I'd agree to spending the night here with Phil. As much as I want to assert my independence and stay at my condo, I can't resist being with him. So, I agree to stay the night here.

"So, Phil, tell me more about the acquisition of your company and the expansion."

"Well, it's not so much an acquisition, but rather a transfer of title. Anyway, after I got back from Africa, my boss expressed his wishes to retire. He's been grooming me to take over for years since his son had no interest in the company. He's a wonderful man and has always been like a second father to me. The past few months, we've been going over the legalities and when I went back, we finalized everything. Being that I found you, I, of course, wanted to be here, close to you. We had looked into expanding before, so the decision was simple. We only needed to find a location. Luckily, I found a great space downtown and leased two floors in the building. It'll take several months to hire staff, train them, and complete the offices, but it's all moving ahead nicely."

"Wow, and do you think you will be able to get enough business out here?"

"You, my dear, lack confidence in me. We have clients all over the country, all over the world, for that matter. This just gives them another outlet to do business with us. Of course, it also lets me find new business. Trust me, this is a great opportunity for me and the company."

"That's great news, Phil, but are you sure you want to uproot your entire life, leave your friends and family, just to be near me?"

"You and Sara are my family. I wouldn't want to be anywhere but here."

Phil takes me in his arms and kisses me; I melt right into his soft, full lips. His hand slides down my side, running down my thigh., I feel myself yearning for him, for more of his touch, yet knowing I can't.

"Phil, I want this so much, but I can't... doctor's orders. But if you're okay with it, maybe we could just cuddle for a while?"

"Baby, I'm so sorry. I didn't even think of it like that. Did I hurt you?"

"No, don't be sorry. I'm fine. The doctor said I need to wait another three weeks before resuming sexual activity."

Laying in his arms, I slightly lift my head and our eyes meet. "Phil, please stay with me tonight."

"I'll stay with you as long as you want me to, baby. I want to hold you till the end of time."

After a few minutes of composing ourselves, we head to the master suite, jump in a hot shower together, and then spend the night in each other's arms. I never want him to leave; I must tell him tomorrow that I want him to stay here... in this room with me... every night. I can't stand to be away from the man I love for even one more night. He completes me more than I ever thought possible.

By, Charlotte Blackwell

Chapter 34

Phil

In the past few weeks since I moved to San Francisco, things have been advancing nicely. Not only has Trista agreed to have me live in the main house with her, she's even asked me to share her bed. I couldn't feel more blessed. We visit Sara at the hospital several times each day; she's getting so big and surpassing all expectations. The doctors actually believe she'll be strong enough to come home before her actual due date, possibly in the next week. They've begun car seat testing to ensure she can maintain her oxygen levels. Just like her mom, she's a fighter. Today they're testing her eyes for something called ROP - Retinopathy of Prematurity - a potentially blinding disorder that affects micro preemies. Her past exams for this condition have been good; today will be her final screening. I'm a little nervous, I'm guessing because it's her last one and she has been doing so well. How did we get so lucky that she hasn't had any real complications yet? We've bonded with other parents, and watched them go through all kinds of troubles. Some babies have even been sent home on oxygen or with a feeding tube and weren't nearly as early as Sara. It's pretty obvious that my late wife Sara is her guardian angel and is making sure that she thrives. Wow... late wife... that's the first time I've thought of Sara in that way. I know that's the proper term, but she's always just been my wife, even though she's deceased. I guess having Trista and our baby is helping me move from understanding to acceptance.

Trista walks in the room looking better than ever. "Are you ready to go? Our sweet angel's waiting for us."

"I'm always ready to see her." I smile as we head to the car.

While driving to the hospital, Trista asks me about work, and how things are coming along. I've been going into the office half days since my relocation and completed all the necessary renovations. This week, I'm beginning the interview process for new staff. A few of my employees from New York have joined me here. A few will stay on only to train new employees, but a couple have decided to relocate as well. We should be fully operational within a month. Things are just falling into place; this is the way it should be.

It only takes a few minutes to arrive at the hospital, and together, the love of my life and I return once again to the NICU where our daughter's been living the past six weeks. It's been a difficult stretch, but Sara is doing great and today, we'll cross one more concern off her list.

As we walk into the NICU, Joanne - one of Sara's nurses - greats us, "Good morning, Trista and Phil, how are you doing today?"

Trista looks up as she performs her scrub. "Hopefully good, but I guess we'll see in a few minutes. How's our little peanut today?"

"Another great night. She passed her car seat test and hasn't needed oxygen all night."

"That's great! Thanks for taking such good care of her," I respond.

"You know, I really believe that starting the kangaroo care so early is what's helped her thrive. Good call on that one, Phil."

"Hey, you never know until you try."

Once our scrubs are complete, we head over to Sara's area. The interns are already at her bedside, discussing her care. Dr. Manning's also present and explains to the interns that today, the pediatric optometrist will be into exam her eyes one last time. He continues by saying they don't expect any changes. Right then, the examining doctor arrives.

"Hello everyone, will we be starting with Sara today? Get our prized pupil out of the way?" She snickers, "Sorry that was a pretty bad pun."

We all laugh and she asks the nurse where they'll be performing the exams today. The charge nurse leads the way, allowing the doctor time to set up and prepare for the exam. We've done this a few times already, so we know what to expect. They'll take Sara into a dark room, and the doctor will put drops in her eyes. Then a small, lighted magnifying glass will be placed right against the eyeball, so the doctor can examine every part of her eye. Sara doesn't like it much, and it breaks my heart to hear her cries from the other side of the door. Trista always takes her into kangaroo care immediately after the exam. We find this the fastest way to calm her when she gets overworked.

"The doctor's ready for her now," announces the charge nurse.

I take baby Sara in my arms and walk with the nurse to the exam room, giving her a small kiss on her perfect little head as I hand her over and sit in the chair across the hall. Sara has grown so much in the six weeks since her birth. She's about four and a half pounds, her skin is normal, and now she looks like a baby, instead of a little alien with tons of tubes and wires. She's also been upgraded to a bassinette, instead of the incubator. I love seeing the advancements she's made.

Most of all, I love those big blue eyes and her eyelashes that go for miles. They remind me of my late wife Sara; they really do have a connection. Maybe I need to take a firearms class and get a gun license; pretty sure I'm gonna need it in a few years.

It doesn't take long before the high pitch screams push through the exam room door. My nerves get the best of me and I begin to pace the hall. I hate her being uncomfortable or sad and wish I could make it all go away for her. Back and forth, I walk the floor looking at my watch and wondering what's taking so long. In the past, it's only been a few minutes, but today it's already been much longer. Trying to convince myself nothing is wrong, I tell myself they are just being thorough since it's her last exam.

The door finally opens, and the nurse walks out with Sara. "Here you go, Phil. The doctor will be over to talk to you and Trista shortly."

Taking my little peanut back to her mommy, who's all ready for her cuddle, I can't help but think that something was different. Whatever... I'm just being silly.

"What's wrong, Phil?" Trista asks, as I undress Sara and place her next to Trista.

"Nothing... it just took longer than usual. Guess it was all the final checks and such."

It doesn't take long for Trista to calm the baby; she loves being in her mommy's arms. I don't blame her, because so do I. I have a feeling that when we get to bring her home, there may be some jealousy over who gets Mommy and when... even though I know Sara will always win.

Not long after Sara settles down, the optometrist and Dr. Manning return. "Hi Trista and Phil, I see you calmed Sara down quickly."

"Yeah, I guess I have the magic touch," Trista jokes.

"Well, we wanted to talk to you about her exam," Dr. Manning says, touching Trista on the shoulder.

My heart sinks, knowing that something's wrong. I felt it this morning and now I know it's true.

The optometrist pulls up a chair next to us. "I'm sorry things took so long today, but I wanted to double check my findings. During my exam today, I discovered Sara has a complete, bilateral retinal detachment. It is considered inoperable here in the States and unfortunately, this means your daughter will likely be blind for the rest of her life. I'm sorry we weren't able to catch it sooner, but sometimes this just happens. Her previous screenings were clear, so I'm quite surprised by today's findings."

Trista begins to sob, and the nurse gently removes Sara from her arms. I swing out of my chair and drop to my knees in front of the woman I love. "Baby, it will be okay, Sara is healthy in every other way. We can do this... SHE can do this.

The Climb

We'll do everything we can for her and find the best schools and specialists. Please, don't worry, baby."

"Don't worry? How can you say that? Our baby will never see colors, she'll never see the sun or the flowers bloom, she'll never see our faces and how much we love her."

"You may be right, but she can experience everything in a different way. She'll hear the beat of our hearts and know that we adore her, she'll feel the sun on her face and know it's shining on her. I know you hurt for our girl, but at least we still have her here with us."

She throws her arms around me and lets out an intense cry into my shoulder. With my hand stroking her back, I try to calm her. I feel her deep breaths going in and out, as she tries to compose herself. My heart is breaking right now for both my girls. I know I need to be strong; I need to be here for them, now and always.

"Trista" Dr. Manning calls out, "Phil is right, my dear. I know it feels like the end of the world right now, but things are still favorable for Sara. Her health is excellent. I've never seen a baby born at her age make it this far without major complications. To be honest, of all the things she could have gone through, this may be the easiest for her to live with. We'll put you in contact with all the appropriate doctors and educational facilities. You are two of the most amazing and dedicated parents I've ever seen come through this nursery, and if anyone can succeed past an obstacle like this, it's your family."

I nod and smile at the doctor that has been here through every struggle, every triumph and couldn't agree more. We're a family of survivors and we'll get through this together.

"Why don't we let the two of you talk. We will be in my office if you have any questions. I'm sorry we can't do more," Dr. Manning comforts.

By, Charlotte Blackwell

Chapter 35

Trista

Looking at Sara, I try to calm myself for her. This isn't something you dream about when you think about having a child. No one wants their children to go through any adversity like blindness. I know it could be worse, but right now, at this very moment, it feels like the end of the world to me.

"Phil, there has to be something we can do. I hate to ask, but you have money and as you've said, money talks. Can you please find out if there's anything that can be done?"

As he tries to comfort me, he nods his head, and with one look at Sara, he says, "I will do anything I can, baby. We'll get a second opinion; we'll travel the world to the best treatment facilities. Money's no object and I don't care if it takes every penny I have, we will exhaust all options for our baby girl."

"God Phil, what kind of life will she have? Will she ever be able to live on her own, hold down a job, find love, and care for a child of her own? I want the world for her, but with one complication it seems like so much is being taken away."

"Trista, don't think like that. There are plenty of able people walking around every day with a disadvantage or disability. Today, people with disabilities have just as many, if not more opportunities offered to them. They might not be the same, but they are great, none the less."

"Disabled… our baby girl's disabled…" I begin to cry again. "Can you call my mom? I need my mom here."

"Anything for you, baby. I'll be right back."

Through tear-glazed eyes, I watch Phil walk down to the visitor waiting room, as I try to picture what Sara's life will be like. How I will read to her and help her with homework. She's going to need to learn braille; do books come in print and braille, or what? Does she need those large sunglasses to protect her and a white stick to feel her way around? So many questions. Oh, no! What about the stairs in the new house? They're a huge danger. She won't be able to see them and could fall and get badly hurt! My mind's racing a mile a minute and I don't even realize that I'm hyperventilating, until nurse Joanne walks over.

"Trista, here... breathe into this paper bag. Honey, it's all going to be okay. You're working yourself up. Now concentrate on your breathing, in and out, nice and slow, deep breath in... okay, now let it out... one, two, three... control it, nice and slow. Good girl, keep it going, you can do it."

I let out a large sigh. "Thanks, Joanne. What am I ever going to do without you once we leave?"

Phil walks in. "Maybe you don't have to find out."

"What do you mean?" I ask.

"Well, I was thinking of hiring a nanny to help you, but what if we hire Joanne? Would you be interested?"

"Actually, I was recently telling my family that the shift work was getting tiring. I'd love to discuss it more with you. Let's talk over lunch one day," Joanne responds with a smile.

"Great! Let's plan for later this week, but for now, the task at hand... Trista, baby, your mom's on her way. Once she arrives, I'll look into possibilities for ROP and talk with the doctors, make sure that we exhaust all our options."

"Phil, I really can't thank you enough. You've stood by me and supported me in every way possible. I love you and will until the end of time."

"I love you too, baby. Now, do you need anything?"

"No, I just want some time alone with Sara until my mom gets here if you both don't mind."

"Not at all. I'll be just a text away, if you need me," Phil says, before leaning down and kissing my head.

Joanne does a quick check on Sara and then takes her chart and heads to the nursing station. Now here I am, alone with my perfect little girl... scared to death about the future. Yet, looking at her and thinking about everything she's already been through, I can't help but feel hopeful. Something Phil said must have gotten through to me... I just can't pinpoint exactly what he said that helped.

I can't believe how my life's changed in less than a year. I thought my trip to Africa would be the highlight of my life. Never in a million years did I expect to meet the love of my life. Then to believe that I had lost him, finding out I was expecting his baby, nearly losing my baby and myself in a car accident, only to have him save us both. Not to mention, the way he's stood by my side through everything, purchased my dream house, uprooted his entire life to be with us. It's all a little overwhelming when I think about it. I really couldn't ask for more. Yet, here I am, praying that he can pull off a miracle and find a way for our daughter to see. I know if he can't, he'll do everything in his power to make life easier for her. I should focus on that... on making sure she's happy.

"Trista, are you still with us?"

"Oh, sorry Mom...I'm just in my own little world. I didn't even hear you come in."

"I figured as much when I called your name a few times. Is everything okay, sweetheart? Phil said you needed me."

"Oh Mom, I don't know. I mean it's not, but it will be, I mean... I just don't know."

"Why don't you just tell me what happened. I love that you still need me, but tell me *why* you need me." She sits next to me, taking my hand in hers.

"Well, today was Sara's last check for the ROP. Unfortunately, since her last exam, her retinas have completely detached in both eyes. She's blind mom, my baby girl is blind." Tears make their way down my cheeks once again.

"Oh kiddo, I understand why you're upset, but look at her. You have a healthy, beautiful, strong girl in front of you and nothing can change that. So, she can't see, but that doesn't mean she won't have the biggest imagination you've ever seen. You can describe things to her, let her feel things around her and she will learn to see without her eyes. This isn't the end of the world; it's just the beginning of a new world for you."

Looking at my mom, I realize she's right... Phil's right. It's just different, not over. "Thanks, Mom. How is it you always know just what to say?"

"Because I'm your mom and I know just what you need. You'll have this gift one day too. You're already a great mom to this little angel and you are going to grow as a parent, and as a person, all because of her."

Chapter 36

Phil

"Excuse me, Dr. Manning?" I call out while knocking on the office door.

"Yes, come in," he announces. "Oh Phil, I'm glad you're here. We were hoping you might come speak with us."

"Well, I didn't want to talk too openly around Trista. She's quite devastated."

"Yes, we felt the same. How are you doing?" he asks.

"I'm doing okay; I have to be, for my girls. I do want to talk to you about options, though. Are you positive there's nothing we can do to help Sara?"

"Well, that's the thing, we didn't want to bring it up right away, because we are unaware of your financial situation and any options would be very pricey. Instead, we decided to look into our possibilities more closely and then come to you and offer options. As we mentioned there's nothing we can do here in the States."

"Well, doctors, let me clear something up. Finances are not an issue. I'm a very wealthy man and nothing, I repeat, nothing will prevent my daughter from getting the best possible care. For that matter, I don't believe a family's financial situation should affect the care they get. Are you saying that if I couldn't afford it, my daughter would be blind because you need to get paid first?" My frustration is growing evident.

"Phil, I'm sorry if you misunderstood me. We have all taken an oath to provide the best care possible, regardless of the ability to pay. What we wanted to do was research options outside of our Country. What I was unsure of is if you could consider international treatment. If you were to get treatment outside of the US, all expenses would be your responsibility. Insurance wouldn't cover anything. There are a few options internationally that may be better alternatives for Sara, but it's not that simple. There's transferring care, transport, medical staffing for transport and then medical expenses out of country. Another option's flying in a different professional, but they may have more specialized equipment where they're from. I'm very sorry if I offended you. We'll offer the best care the United States has to offer for Sara."

"Thank you, Doctor. I think my emotions got the best of me. Please tell me what all our options are for Sara. I want to give her the best chance possible."

The other doctor, Dr. Steeks, begins to explain, "First and foremost, to give your daughter the best chances of correcting the retinal detachment, we must act fast. The sooner surgery's performed the better. I've contacted my mentor, Dr. Masomati, in Italy. I wanted to have options for you, in case we were able to move forward. He's available to perform the surgery day after tomorrow. He needs to know within the next few hours if we plan to move ahead so that he can book the necessary staff and operating room, recovery, and so on. He also needs ten thousand dollars for a down payment. Then, we need to secure a medical team to fly with Sara to Italy as soon as possible. A private medical jet will also be needed; this will cost about a hundred thousand dollars. That covers the jet, pilot, medical staff and equipment for transport. All in all, you can expect to pay in the area of half to three-quarters of a million dollars, possibly double that. Now, the surgical procedures that need to be performed on your daughter are a scleral buckling or a vitrectomy. Another option that may be worth adding to her procedure is a stem cell treatment. It's fairly new but has had some great results. As with any surgery, there are risks of infection and reactions to the anesthetic. It's not guaranteed, either; this is just her best chance. I'd say it's a fifty-fifty shot right now. The surgeon will attempt to repair the blood vessels behind the eyes and repair any damage done. She'll probably never have perfect eyesight, but it may be correctable with prescription lenses. She'll also need continuous follow-up care. We do have treatment centers here, but I'll admit, others are far more advanced."

"Well, let's do it! A fifty percent chance is better than no chance. Here's my platinum card. Do whatever is necessary," I insist, throwing my credit card on the desk.

"Phil, you must understand; there are other risks as well. Sara's still small and although she's been making great advancements, flying her halfway across the world may be dangerous," Dr. Manning warns.

"So then, what will it cost for the two of you to be on her private medical team when we are transferring her?"

"I don't think that's necessary. The transport staff is better trained to treat while in flight. There's a neo-natal doctor that will accompany Sara."

"Very well, let's set it up. May Trista and I travel with Sara and the team?"

"Yes, that will be fine. I will make the referral and have arrangements made. Why don't you go home and pack, and meet us back here in three hours? "

I thank the doctors and race back to Sara's side. Trista and I will need to prepare now. I will have to meet with Joanne at a later date.

"Hi Katherine, I'm glad you made it. How are you ladies doing?" I ask, trying not to appear rushed or panicked.

"Better... Mom always knows just how to set me in my place. What about you, did you find anything out?" Trista allows a small grin to sneak out.

"Well, I may have some good news. Dr. Steeks knows an Italian doctor that can operate on Sara. There's no guarantee, but it could give her a fifty percent chance of regaining her sight."

"That's amazing, babe! I knew you could do it. When does he work, is he here now?" Trista's eyes light up with excitement and promise.

"I should have been more specific. He's in Italy, and we have to take Sara to him. We leave in three hours. Let's go pack and I will explain everything. Katherine, would you like to come back to the house and get the details as well? We have to meet the team back here, so you can pick up your car then."

"Sounds good, thank you, Phil. Everyone say 'see you soon' to peanut, and let's go. You don't have much time.

By, Charlotte Blackwell

Chapter 37

Trista

Everything's happening so fast. Thank God, Sara's paperwork got here this week. I can't believe we are thirty thousand feet in the air and on route to Italy. This plane's like a traveling hospital; I never even knew things like this existed. I don't even want to think about what this is costing Phil. God, once we get back home, I'm never going to see him. He's gonna have to work the next fifty years straight just to pay for everything. I'm going to have to live a hundred lifetimes to thank him.

    I have to admit that I'm a little nervous. Here we are, high in the sky with our little peanut. She wasn't even ready to come home, yet here she's on her first international flight. I never expected to see Rome, and now I'm putting my daughter's future in the hands of a doctor there... one I know very little about. This is going to be the longest fourteen hours of my life.

    The aircraft is huge and beautiful. The medical area's only part of the plane. When we boarded, the flight attendant gave us a tour; there's a rest area, a comfortable seating area where we can enjoy movies and dinner and then, of course, the medical area. This is exactly what I imagine a private plane to look like. I guess the medical team's only allowed eight-hour shifts while in flight, so they take turns and go to sleep in the rest area, where there are several sound-reduced rooms with beds. I'm so grateful for every staff member here. I just wish I knew what to do with my time. The medical area doesn't offer much room for visiting with all the equipment and staff, so I don't really want to be back there, getting underfoot while they're caring for Sara.

    Phil and I relax with a movie in the huge, plush leather chairs, which is kinda turning into our thing. He's so insightful and loves discussing the film after we've watched it. He really encourages me to expand my mind and thought process. I love being challenged.

"Hey baby, whatcha thinking?" Phil reaches over and brushes my hand.
"Nothing much... just life and how things have changed."
"Well, I think life's great, now that we are together."
"I couldn't agree more," I say, while moving over to the man of my dreams to sit on his lap.
"Now this is what I call in-flight entertainment," he jokes.
"Shut up and kiss me, you goofball."
Like a good man, Phil does as he's told, and presses his lips to mine. With a small swipe of his tongue, one hand on my hip and one at the back of my head, I melt right into him. He pulls me in as close as possible. Running my hands through his hair as we kiss makes me want him even more.
"Baby, you better be careful, or I won't be able to resist myself. I just might rip your clothes off right here." His eyes are filled with love and passion.
"Oh, how I'd love that hun, but we have to remain focused," I resolve.
"You're right, but I'm not gonna lie, this trip might include a little excitement for us, too, so be prepared," he teases. I bury my head in his shoulder and whisper, "I love you."
"I love you too, baby. Guess you should get off my lap before the flight staff walks in."
Unable to control my laughter, I climb off him and readjust my outfit. Once we're both presentable again, I sit next to him and we watch the movie. Having his arms around me makes me melt, and I know this is as close to heaven as a girl can get. I give a soft kiss to his neck and rest my head on his shoulder.

∞ ∞ ∞

As the plane descends into Rome, I feel a sense of relief that Sara's made it through the flight without incident. Within a few short hours, she'll be ready for surgery. I just hope it's a success and she'll have at least a chance of having sight.
The sun's just rising in Italy. It's beautiful here, with its old architecture and history. It would be lovely to vacation here one day. As the plane touches down, I can see the medical team waiting on the tarmac and it hits me; my baby girl's going in for surgery. I pray that she handles it well. After all, she shouldn't have even been born yet. The seat belt light goes off, and both Phil and I proceed to the medical area of the plane. The medical team has already begun attaching Sara to portable monitors. The exit door opens, and they proceed down the ramp with my baby girl. I

By, Charlotte Blackwell

watch as the new medical team takes the report and loads her into the ambulance. Rushing down behind them, Phil and I jump in the town car waiting for us. We'll follow them to the hospital, check her in, and if there are no delays, surgery should be in the next few hours. The excitement and nerves begin to affect me, and I feel as if my heart will pound right out of my chest. Phil squeezes my hand and his touch comforts me. I'm so grateful he's here. My emotions are in hyper-drive, and I can only focus on Sara, not the world around me… not this beautiful country.

Chapter 38

Phil

I wish there was something I could do to calm Trista, as she paces back and forth across the hospital floor. Sara's been in surgery for an hour and a half already, and we're just waiting for someone to come give us news. Dr. Masomati was very optimistic when we met him upon our arrival. He walked us through the procedure, the risks, and recovery. I have full confidence in his abilities, but all I can do is hope it will work out for the best.

"Trista, baby, come sit down. Sara is going to be just fine. Relax a little; remember the power of positive thinking."

She inhales deep and sits next to me. "I can't help it. That's our baby girl in there. What's taking so long? He said it would only be about an hour and we are closing in on two."

"I'm sure he's just taking his time because she's so small."

Right then, the doctor walks out. "I'm glad you are both here. Sorry for the wait."

"Thank you, Doctor. How's Sara doing?" I ask.

"She is stable, but we did have some complications during surgery."

"Oh, God." Trista cries.

"Miss Smith, everything is okay, Sara is fine and in recovery. The eye surgery went fine, but because of her prematurity, we had difficulty with her respirations and she went into respiratory arrest. The team was able to revive her and she's resting nicely. She's on oxygen, but should recover quickly."

"Okay, we can handle this. Will she be able to see?" Trista questions through her tears.

"We won't know until she's healed, but it looks very promising," the surgeon encourages.

"When can we see her?" I ask.

"As soon as she's moved from recovery to the ICU; why don't you go get a bite to eat and take a breather? There is a wonderful café across the street. When you get back, she should be settled on the unit."

Taking the doctor's orders, I encourage Trista out of the hospital and we head to the traditional Italian café across the street. Outside is a canopy, covering several little two-seater tables scattered across the patio, all surrounded by greenery. An open and inviting door allows the heavenly scent of fresh pasta and breads to waft into the street. We follow the tantalizing aroma and a robust, olive-skinned woman invites us to sit at a table near an open window by the street. The scent of garlic and cheese explodes from the kitchen. I have a feeling I may gain a little weight during this trip.

"Welcome, welcome, please, sit... eat. Here's some bread. You dip it in the olive oil and balsamic sauce. It's good, yeah?" The woman encourages, with her heavy Italian accent.

"Yes, thank you."

"You come from America?" She smiles.

"Yes, it's our first time here," I return.

"Oh good, good. Here, you drink wine in Italy." She pours us each a small glass of red wine. The strong wood and berry aroma tickles my nose as I breathe in.

I've never felt so welcomed in a restaurant before. I ask her to bring us anything she recommends. Once she places our order, she returns and sits with us. After talking a little, she questions why Trista appears so stressed while on vacation. We explain our situation, and that this isn't a holiday, but that we are here for medical treatment for our newborn baby. Almost instantly, she hugs us both and makes an announcement to everyone within earshot. Every person in sight bows their head and prays; even those passing by on the street pause for a moment. Then collectively, they say "Benedici il bambino. Amen." She tells us it means *bless the child*.

My heart pauses briefly at the power of faith here. I know this is the holy land, but I never thought I'd feel the impact of the Lord I was unsure even existed.

"My children, we pray for your baby, she be healthy now." And with that, the woman continues on with her duties, leaving us to eat.

I've never tasted anything so wonderful before. The fresh-made pasta is heavenly and the atmosphere puts both Trista and I at ease; at least for a few moments. Once we finish our meal and the wine, I ask for our bill and the woman informs us another guest has picked up our tab and wishes our baby girl well. I can't believe this place. We haven't even been here a day and I've never felt so welcome. We thank everyone as we leave and decide to take a short walk around the block before we make our way back to the hospital.

This city's incredible. The streets are immaculate, trees and flowers everywhere, old stone buildings create an incredible ambiance, and you can feel the love in the air. We walk hand in hand down the well-maintained street, watching couples stroll together, seeing the sights and taking in everything Rome has to offer in the few short blocks we stroll. Maybe one day we can come back here with Sara and enjoy it for different reasons.

It only takes minutes for us to arrive back at the large white building where Sara's being treated. It's warm and comforting, nothing like the hospitals back home; more like a movie set in Hollywood. Everything's so crisp and clean, the air smells fresh, and I feel optimistic about Sara's outcome.

"You ready to see our little peanut?"

"I'm so ready, Phil. This has been the longest few hours of my life, and I just want to hold her close to me."

We get to the ICU and are greeted immediately. Just like the staff in the NICU back home, the staff here appears to love what they do. I have the feeling it's more than a paycheck to them; it's that they care about helping people. They take us right to Sara's bedside; she looks peaceful, asleep in her crib. There are monitors hooked up to her once again, like when she was first born. An IV bag hangs beside her, clear liquid running through the tubing placed in her tiny little arm, neatly wrapped and protected. They have a funny little plastic tent over her head; the nurse informs us it's an oxygen tent. They believe it's better for little ones than the nasal tubing. I never wanted to see her hooked up to all this equipment again, but this time I'm more hopeful and believe it will improve her quality of life. Sara's eyes are covered by white gauze patches, protecting them and allowing them to rest from surgery.

"Oh Phil, she looks so fragile."

"Baby, I've said it before and I'll say it again… she's a fighter."

By, Charlotte Blackwell

Chapter 39

Trista

Sitting in the nursery with Sara in my arms is a dream come true. I swear, there were times I thought this day would never come; my sweet little girl, at home and in her own room. Since we returned from Italy almost two months ago, things have been flying at lightning speed. Sara's almost four months old - a whole month past her expected due date. She's gaining weight at a steady pace and is closing in on double digits. So far, her surgery's been a success, but she goes for more tests tomorrow. I can feel in my heart that it's all going to be perfect, just the way she looks at me when she's in my arms. I know she can see me, and I know she sees her daddy because of the grin on her little porcelain face when he walks in the door after work.

"Trista, you better go get ready for your date with Phil. I'll take Sara for you." Joanne says as she comes into the nursery.

"Just a few more minutes... I can't get enough of this little girl."

"I totally understand. Thank you so much for hiring me on as her private nurse. I feel so lucky...I love having the freedom and rewards of caring for one perfect little princess."

"Joanne, it's us that are lucky. You've been with her from the moment she entered this world. You saved her life more than once and encouraged me to believe. We're so blessed to have you as part of our lives."

"Well, thank you none the less, Trista. Now hand over Peanut. Phil called and said to make sure you're ready by five."

"Fine, here you go. I wonder what that man has planned for tonight. He never does anything simple and insists on treating me like royalty, no matter where we go," I chuckle.

"I've never seen a man love a woman the way he loves you. One day I hope to find a love like yours."

"You will, Joanne, and yes, I'm pretty lucky."

With Sara in good hands, I jump in the shower and begin to prepare for our date. Washing my hair, I think about the great memories we've created together. The many times he's pinned me against this shower wall and made love to me. Leaning against the ceramic tile, I wish that he'd barge in and surprise me right this moment. As I run the loofa over my body, my heart starts beating faster, think of him, the man I love. I turn the water a tad cooler - I don't have time for fantasizing... I have to get ready. After a moment, I reach up and shut off the water.

Once out of the shower, I head into the large walk-in closet and on the bench, notice a large white box wrapped in a red ribbon. Dropping my towel to the floor, I race to the box and open it. A small note sits on top of the contents and reads, 'To my love, I thought you might help make this dress look even more beautiful. Tonight's for you, the family you've given me, and showing me that I can fall in love every day. See you soon, my princess. All my love, Phil.'

Tugging at the tissue paper, a red satin gown is revealed. I lift it from the box to get a better look; the neck is a low V-cut, and the floor-length gown has a high slit that comes right to the hip. Wow! Phil thinks I can pull off this beautiful gown? I had better do something with my hair. I toss on my terry robe and race to the bathroom. Putting the blow dryer on high, I dry my hair as fast as possible; a little tease here and there, and then I smooth it out into a clean, low pony with a slight bump on top, sweeping my bangs to the side. Pleased with the quick style, I begin working on my make-up.

My phone starts vibrating, and I notice a text from Phil. 'On my way, baby. Hope you're almost ready. Can't wait for tonight.' I race back into the closet, pulling on a thong and one of those low cut bras before slipping into the gown. I dig around, looking for the perfect pair of shoes and see a box I don't recognize. Peeking inside, I see a pair of silver sling-back heels, encrusted with rhinestones, in my size. A little giggle sneaks out; this man thinks of everything. I turn to my jewelry cabinet and open the top drawer, looking for a suitable pair of earrings. This time, I find a blue velvet box covering the entire area of the drawer. I open it to find a beautiful diamond necklace, and hanging earrings, each link connecting like leaves on a wreath. How did I ever get so lucky?

The chime as the front door opens lets me know Phil's arrived. With one last glance in the mirror, I walk towards the staircase with confidence I never thought I'd have. Standing at the top, I reach for the railing and begin my descent to the man standing at the bottom step, waiting for me with his grin reaching ear-to-ear. I feel blessed, as if I'm living a fairytale.

"My god, woman, I knew you were beautiful... but... but... I don't know if we will make it to our dinner reservations." His eyes glistening, as he watches every step I take toward him. "You are far too good to me. I think I've mentioned this a time or ten before." As I reach the last step, Phil reaches his hand out to me, guiding me right into his arms.

"My love, you deserve the world." He pulls me close and dips me, pressing his lips to mine. "I could take you right now, right here on these stairs."

"As much as I'd love that, I can't allow this dress to go to waste."

He smiles and places my wrap over my shoulders. Arm-in-arm, we walk out through the front door. That's when I see the white stretch limo parked in front. A short, stout man in full chauffeur dress waits with the door open wide. Together, we take a seat in the back. Small white lights line the inside, and a fully stocked bar, complete with a bottle of champagne on ice awaits us. Phil takes the flutes and fills them, handing me one. We clink glasses and take a sip before he leans towards me and kisses me again. I love the feeling of his lips against mine. Even when he's not with me, I still feel their lingering caress.

After a short drive downtown, we arrive at the best restaurant in the city. I've never eaten here before, but it gets great reviews and reservations must be made months in advance. Phil must have been planning this night for a while now. As we walk in, the hostess greets us and immediately leads us to our table. It's magnificent in here; crisp white and black linens, and candles on every table. There's a large water fountain made from clear glass tiles, perfectly situated on the guest side of the kitchen. When we get to our seats in the back, where it's quiet and more private, the waiter meets us with a bottle of wine. Presenting it to Phil, he smiles and nods with approval. The waiter pours us each a glass before placing the bottle in the ice bucket to the side of the table.

"I hope you don't mind, Trista, but I placed our order earlier today."

"I trust you, Phil. This is beautiful; I can't wait to try the cuisine."

"I've heard amazing things about this place. I'm sure we'll have a lovely dinner."

Over the next ninety minutes, course after course is brought out to us. If I eat one more thing, I'll burst out of this dress. It feels like a second skin, but I'm sure it isn't very forgiving if I overeat. I've never eaten raw meat before, but the beef sashimi was delicious, and the dandelion salad, who would have thought. Of course, my favorite was our main course of orange glazed duck... another thing I never thought I'd enjoy.

"So, do you approve? I hope everything was to your liking," Phil asks.

"Yes, of course, but why so formal?"

"Sorry, I guess the ambiance just put me informal mode." He laughs. "I hope you're ready for dessert."

"Oh Phil, I don't know if I can handle one more bite..."

The waiter presents a fluffy chocolate mousse before I can finish my sentence.

"Okay, maybe a few bites… you know I can't resist chocolate." I smile before scooping up a spoonful.

By, Charlotte Blackwell

Chapter 38

Phil

I think tonight's a complete success. I hope Trista realizes that she means the world to me and deserves everything. Back in the limo, Trista thinks we're just going home, but I have other plans. I haven't really gotten to see the sights since moving here. Between Sara, getting the house ready, and getting the business off the ground, my days have been jam-packed. Tonight's the first night Trista and I've really gotten out. My plan's to go to the Golden Gate Bridge. I hear it's a magnificent sight. I've learned that Trista really enjoys architecture, so I hope she'll enjoy this as much as I will.

"I thought we were going home? Why are we heading towards the mainland?" she questions.

"I just figured since we have the night out, we may as well see some sights. I haven't had the chance yet. Is that alright?" I smirk.

"Of course, Phil, I'm sorry. I just feel a little awkward leaving Sara."

"I understand, but you deserve a night off too. You're with her all the time since you left your job to be a full-time mom."

"I want to thank you again for that, I mean taking on the burden of financially supporting both Sara and me."

"Baby, what are you talking about? You are my girls. It's no burden; it's my duty to provide for you. Sorry if that sounds a little chauvinistic. Just call me old-fashioned. Besides, I enjoy taking care of you."

"I appreciate that so much, Phil. It's just hard for me because I've never pictured myself to be the girl that needed a man to take care of her."

"You do know that you take care of me too, right? You healed me. You are turning me into the best possible man I can be. You do just as much for me as I do for you. We balance each other out. I think maybe I should tell you something."

"That doesn't sound good."

The Climb

"You seem to be concerned with finances, and I really want you to know that we don't have to worry. I come from a very privileged family, but I also make my own money."

"I know you do, but eventually, it's going to run out."

"That's the thing, sweetheart... it won't. My family has billions. Not to mention, last year alone, I made $50 million dollars, so the money isn't going to run out, honey. I can take care of our family and anything either of my girls want."

Trista just sits there with a look of complete and utter shock. I don't know what to do, so I lean over and kiss her.

She pulls back just slightly and says, "Let me get this straight, you are a multi-millionaire... and your family... billionaires?"

"Yeah, that's right."

"So, answer me this. What on earth do you want with me? I don't have anything to offer you; I'm not a trophy girlfriend. I just don't get it. You could have any woman in the world, yet you choose me."

I just smile as the limo comes to a stop on the side of the bridge, and our driver walks around to open the door.

"What's going on? You want to get out in the middle of the bridge? I don't know if we're allowed to do this, Phil." She looks at me with confused eyes.

"Don't worry; I've taken care of everything... and will you stop being so hard on yourself?" I smile, "come on, let's go see the view."

As we step out, Trista gasps at the sight. The bridge is fully lit and the skyline's on fire, with all the lights from the city reflecting off the water. It's almost as beautiful as she is.

As we walk hand in hand down the side, Trista looks over the edge to the water. "This is perfect, Phil. Thank you for bringing me out here."

With her hand in mind, I stop and turn to her. Dropping on to one knee, I look up at the love that has completed me. She raises her hand to her mouth and tears begin to fall down her cheeks.

"Trista, from the day I met you, I knew there was something different about you. I was drawn to you; I needed to know you, needed to be with you. When we came back from Africa, I thought I had lost you forever; my heart broke a little more every day. It seemed that the universe was against us, but instead, it proved that what is meant to be, will be. We've been through more than most couples go through in a lifetime, and every day, I love you more. I promised you that one day, I would make you my wife when the time was right, and I believe that time is now. Trista, if you do me the extreme honor of becoming my wife, I promise to love you forever and be with you as all our dreams come true. Will you marry me?" From my coat pocket, I pull out a ring box, opening it to present a five-carat, emerald-cut diamond ring. The platinum band is covered with dozens of smaller diamonds. My heart's beating faster than ever, as I wait for her answer.

I see the light reflecting off the tears in her eyes, as a smile beams from the corners of her mouth, which is hidden behind her hand. Thankfully, she nods. "Yes, yes I'll marry you!"

I rise in front of her while placing the ring on her finger; her hands are shaking. Giving them a little squeeze, I try to calm her. Kissing the finger that now carries a small token of the love I have for her, I pull her close and kiss her harder and with more passion than ever before. The cars surrounding us on the bridge have all come to a stop, and begin honking and flashing their high beams at us. Screams come from cars everywhere, "Congrats," people holler, one after another. Trista starts to laugh, and buries her head in my shoulder; I can feel the heat from her cheeks as they burn with embarrassment.

"I love you, baby. Thank you for making me the happiest man on the planet."

"I love you, too, and thank you for making me feel like a princess."

"You are a princess… my princess… and I'll make sure you know that every day for the rest of our lives."

∞ ∞ ∞

Back at the house, Trista opens the door and I sweep her off her feet, taking her in my arms and whispering, "I need to practice for our wedding night."

The house is quiet, so I assume Joanne has Sara down for the night. I carry Trista up the stairs to our room. Placing her feet on the floor, her back is facing me. Her neck, long and slender, shoulders smooth and perfect, I can't resist any longer. Kissing the nape of her neck, I take down the zipper of her gown, letting it drop to the floor. She tips her head and arches her back, making her chest stand out. I reach around the front of her, caressing her bare skin. Her black bra and thong drive me wild. Kissing her neck, I reach her mouth as she leans back into me. She reaches her hand around and unbuckles my belt, and as my pants fall, I step out of them so as not to get tangled. Trista tugs at me, pulling me toward our bed. Knowing we will finally make love once again, my excitement grows.

"Trista, baby, I love you."

"I love you too, Phil," she whispers.

The Climb

Slow and steady, with love and passion, I make love to my future wife, mother of my child and the reason for my existence. After falling asleep in each other's arms, knowing that life is the way it should be, I know with all certainty, this is true happiness.

By, Charlotte Blackwell

Chapter 39

Trista

Today we meet with the eye specialist to evaluate Sara's eyes. I know in my heart that the surgery was a success; there's no way she'd look at me the way she does if she couldn't see. Phil and I are so grateful for our baby girl, and how well she has adjusted. Some of the parents we met in the hospital haven't been as blessed. Some have lost their babies, others have needed multiple and complex surgeries to save their children. I feel like we escaped, barely scathed. Thinking back to the way I acted when I learned she had ROP, I feel ridiculous; of everything that could have happened to her, ROP is probably the least serious.

"Sara McKay and parents, please follow me," the medical assistant calls out.

We follow her into the back exam room, and she notifies us that the doctor will be in shortly. We literally just sit down and he's in the room.

"Good afternoon, my name is Dr. Glenn. I understand that Sara's been transferred to my care for follow-up after surgery to correct her ROP."

Phil responds, "Yes, Doctor. She had surgery two months ago in Italy."

"Why don't we get her up on the exam table, so we can take a peek."

Phil carries Sara over to the table and lays her down. The assistant wraps her tightly in a blanket so that she can't move or put her hands on her face. The doctor then places a few drops in her eyes and turns the room lights off. Pulling out the lighted magnifying tool, he places it in front of one eye and then the next. It takes all of thirty seconds, and they turn the lights on dim. I begin to get nervous because of how fast he examined her.

"Well that was easy; I can see the surgery was a perfect success. Now watch as I shine my penlight."

The Climb

He takes a small flashlight from his coat and shines it at her, moving it side to side. We all watch as Sara follows the light. Not for long, but enough to prove that she sees it. Phil and I embrace each other, and I start to cry happy tears.

"You have a real fighter on your hands, but I'm sure you've heard that before. From what I was told and according to her medical records, your daughter had a fifth-degree retinal detachment. That's the worst possible scenario. In most cases, surgery allows for minimal vision correction, but in Sara's case, it appears that she may have total restoration. This only happens in one out of a thousand cases, so I guess you can consider it a miracle."

"We know that already Doctor; she has a guardian angel watching over her," I say with a smile.

I really have to believe that Phil's late wife, Sara, is watching over us. It was Sara that brought Phil and I together in Africa. I also believe it had to be Sara that brought Phil to me right when I needed him most, so he could save mine and baby Sara's life. Most of all, I know she's watching over our beautiful baby, and helping her live on as our little miracle. I just wish I could thank her.

"So why don't we do another checkup around her first birthday? Of course, if you have any questions or concerns, please call the office. It has been great meeting you and your daughter."

"Thank you so much, Dr. Glenn. We appreciate your help." Phil holds his hand out to shake.

∞ ∞ ∞

I'm so excited the weekend's finally here; Phil's parents and former in-laws are coming in today to finally meet the baby and me. Little do they know, we have a surprise for them... our impending nuptials. Mom and Dad are planning a little dinner party for the family's arrival; I can't wait to tell everyone about Phil proposing. Hiding it from my family has been so difficult, but we want to surprise everyone at the same time.

While Phil goes to the airport, Mom and Dad are busy in my kitchen, preparing tonight's meal. I'm so nervous to meet his family and to introduce Sara to them. Trying to make sure I look perfect, I decide to step away from the mirror for a moment and help Joanne get Sara dressed. We found this great little shop that has the cutest petite baby clothes. I got her the sweetest little pink, frilly dress. I want her dressed to the nines to meet her family. She's even got enough hair to put little pigtails in - really little, but it's super cute. Sara makes me so happy and I'm thrilled that Phil and I get to share this together.

"Trista, you look amazing," Joanne gushes.

"You think? I don't know if this is what I should wear." I fiddle with my outfit.

"It's perfect! That is the cutest skirt... it reminds me of a southern belle or something. And your top goes perfect with it. You look fantastic. Besides, they are going to love you for you. You're the kindest person I've ever met. You always put others before yourself."

I look down at the flowing, flare-set skirt I threw on; it is kinda cute. It's white with black embroidery near the bottom and reaches just below my knees. I paired it with a fitted blouse with three-quarter length, slit sleeves. I guess I kinda *do* look like a southern belle, heels and all. Then I start thinking about her compliment and say, "What are you talking about? Practically since the moment you met me, I've been a blubbering fool, worried about everything. I don't think I've cried as much in my entire life as I have the past year. God, it must be Phil. He brings out emotions I didn't even think I had. I was this strong, independent woman and he has made me this vulnerable crazy person." Then I think to myself... no, I wasn't really strong... I have been an insecure mess for years.

Joanne bursts out laughing. "Of course, he does! You've found someone that you love, and who gives you the world. That would make anyone vulnerable because you don't want to lose him. You also have a comfort with him; you don't have to hide your emotions. It makes perfect sense."

"I guess, I just don't like being vulnerable."

"Trista, you're also forgetting that virtually right after you met Phil, you got pregnant. You have had so many hormones running through your system. Not to mention the accident, and having a severely premature baby... God, that would send most women over the edge. Your hormones will start leveling off soon, and I'd bet my job, you will feel better."

"Please, don't bet your job on anything! I can't lose you."

"You'll always have me as a friend, but you're not going to need a home care nurse forever."

"I might, who knows," I joke.

We both giggle and finish getting Sara ready before heading downstairs. The smell of the dinner Mom's cooking is wafting through the house. I guess I should go help her. It's not fair that she comes and cooks this big meal. I don't get why she just wouldn't let our chef prepare it. Old fashioned, I guess. I, on the other hand, have grown quite accustom to the staff here. I love that I get to play with Sara and take her out during the day, instead of cooking and cleaning all day. Phil really has shown me the good life. It's a huge difference from my old life of saving for every little thing and living paycheck to paycheck. I still can't believe he has all this money and wants to take care of me. Maybe I should think about telling him about my past. He's always said he doesn't understand my insecurities but has never pushed me to explain where they came from. God, I love that man.

By, Charlotte Blackwell

Chapter 40

Phil

I've never seen Trista so nervous before. I know my parents and Sara's parents will love her. I mean, how many new girlfriends would accept a man's deceased wife's family as her own? She's so understanding and even if she doesn't believe so, confident and secure. I have yet to find anything that I don't love and appreciate about her. Well, maybe the fact that she's so hard on herself and squeezes the toothpaste from the middle of the tube instead of the end, but it's no deal breaker.

The moment I come home from the airport with my family, they fall just as in love as I am. Mom's smile could reach the moon, and everyone takes turns grabbing Trista for a hug. It doesn't take long for every person that's important to me to fall in love with one another. I couldn't be happier. Naturally, when they meet baby Sara, well let's just say the tears flow. Before long, dinner's ready and we all sit in the large, formal dining room to enjoy the feast. Trista's brother and his family also join us.

As we all sit around the dinner table and enjoy the amazing roast beef dinner Trista and her mom prepared, we fill in my family about all the events of the past several months. We didn't want them to come meet Sara until she was healthy. I didn't think the mom's would be able to handle seeing her hooked up to all the machines.

"We are so blessed that Phil has found you, Trista, and thank you for giving us such an amazing granddaughter," Mom says.

Trista smiles. "Oh, you don't need to thank me; I should be thanking you for raising such an amazing man. Although, you should really tell him to stop spoiling me so much! He's far too good to me."

"You ladies need to stop all this mush. We're wonderful together, Trista," I wink, hinting we should announce our engagement.

"I'll give you that, we're perfect together."

Katherine jumps in, "So maybe you should just tell us...."

"Excuse me? Tell you what?" Trista perks up.

"Trista, you are living together, have a beautiful daughter and are perfect together. We all know it's going to happen sooner or later." Katherine confirms it's time for us to make it official.

I stand, taking my wine glass in my hand. "Well, it appears you are hinting at something, so I'd like to announce that Trista has agreed to become my wife."

Everyone claps and hugs, and then Dad looks at me and laughs.

"What's so funny, Dad?"

"Well Son, we all knew. Apparently, you have no idea, though."

"How did you know? And no idea about what?" I question.

They all laugh and Dad says, "Your proposal was recorded and went viral online. It's even been on the news. Your driver that night recorded and posted the entire thing."

"Are you serious?" Trista covers her face in embarrassment.

"Sweetie, we all knew days after it happened, and it's being deemed the most romantic proposal of the year," my late wife's mom says, with excitement.

After dinner, while all the parents visit one another and baby Sara, Trista and I go online to see what they are talking about. We are amazed, as we find our video has over 5 million hits on YouTube. There have even been parody videos made. Reading all the comments and well wishes warms us. The best ones are from the men planning on proposing, and giving me hell because they will never be able to top this.

Katherine comes to the office. "Will you two stop goofing around and join us, please?"

With a smile, we both follow orders and retreat to the living room with the family.

My mom takes the lead. "So now that you have officially told us about your impending marriage, can we start discussing the wedding? Have you set a date?"

"We haven't talked much about it. Maybe we should figure out what works with everyone's schedules," Trista replies, with a sense of responsibility.

"The sooner the better for me." I admit, "I can't wait to make you my wife."

"Well, I guess we need to decide some things... like how big of a wedding do we want, where do we want it, are we going to do everything or hire a planner?" Trista questions.

Mom pipes up, "I think it should be a good size wedding; we have lots of family, friends and business associates from New York, plus, of course, all *your* friends and family. We are more than happy to help with the planning and financial aspects of the wedding."

"Mom's right, I do have many people that I should invite. Are you alright with a bigger wedding?"

"Honestly, the only thing that matters to me is our marriage. I've never been one of those 'girlie-girls' that planned their wedding from the day they could walk."

"Trista, you must have *some* ideas though," Dad interjects.

"Well, I have an idea about the dress I want, I'd love to have calla lilies and roses, and of course, my friend Katie as my maid of honor. Other than that, I don't really know. I never expected to find someone that I'd want to marry. I hate to add more expense, as weddings are costly enough, but I would love the assistance of a wedding planner. If we're going to have a big wedding, someone should know what they are doing."

"Oh Trista, you are our only daughter. Dad and I would be happy to cover the expense of a planner," Katherine interjects.

"I assume you'd like to enjoy a honeymoon on your own, so planning will also depend on when you will be comfortable enough to leave Sara with someone while you vacation," Mom suggests.

"I think we are both comfortable with that anytime, as long as Joanne is involved in her care. Joanne knows her schedule, has the medical training and knows her health care providers." Trista smiles at Joanne, looking for approval.

With excitement, I make a suggestion, "I can't wait for our wedding, so how would you all feel about doing it this coming May? It's a beautiful time of year."

"That's only a few months away! Do you really think a large wedding can be planned in that amount of time?" Trista asks with surprise.

"Trista, my dear, we can do anything we set our minds to. We just need to find a planner who is up for the task," Mom insists.

"What about venues and such? We may not be able to book on such short notice."

I smile, "What about having the wedding here? The vineyard will make a beautiful setting, and we certainly have the room."

Everyone agrees that a spring wedding here is perfect. We decide to start scheduling interviews with planners tomorrow, and everyone can be involved in the preparations. We'll need to work fast, but since Trista's home and Joanne's here to help, I'm sure they will be able to make things happen. We decide on Memorial Day weekend, as this gives guests that are traveling more time off, without having to use up extra vacation days.

Chapter 41

Trista

I can't believe it's here; today Phil and I will marry. I miss him already since he spent last night at the Ritz-Carlton. Tonight we'll stay there together for our wedding night. The vineyard has been transformed, a beautiful white tent assembled, and I feel like royalty with the wedding we have planned.

Last night, Katie stayed over, and we had a girl's night in, including Joanne. She's become one of my best friends and agreed to be my bridesmaid. Phil had a mobile spa sent to the house and we were pampered with facials, massages, mani-pedi's, and more. The hair stylist and make-up artist should be arriving soon to get us pretty enough to be presentable. As we rise to the beautiful morning, Joanne insists on working and is already off to tend to Sara. Chef sends up a hearty breakfast of eggs benedict, fruit, coffee, and mimosa's.

"I can see how you could get used to this, Trista. My God, this man is good to you," Katie gushes.

"Yeah, I've got it good; the love of a great man, a beautiful daughter, amazing friends, and so much more. I really don't understand what I did to deserve such a great life."

"You were just you; a good friend, an amazing mother, and I assume from your stories, a great lover. What more could a man want?"

"Thanks, Katie, I love you."

"I love you too, Trista. Now let's get you ready. We should do everything except get your dress on so that your hair and makeup won't mess the dress when they're done."

The time is flying by so fast and before we know it, our 'primpers,' as we started calling them, arrive. Allowing them to do my hair as they see fit, I sit in the chair, away from the mirror so that I can be surprised. I feel them tugging and pulling my hair back, twisting and braiding and I can't wait to see what they come up with. The make-up people work on Katie, and then call Joanne in to have hers done. My heart begins to pound, as it sinks in that in just a few hours, I'll be Phil's wife. Wow, we've been through so much this past year. Oh my God, I didn't even realize until this very moment... it's the anniversary of our climb in Africa! He must have planned it that way. That's why he wanted the wedding this weekend! What a romantic he is.

There's a gentle rap on the door, "Come in," I call out.

Mom comes in. "Good morning. How's my girl feeling?"

"Excited, I can't wait."

"Well, you have a man that can't wait either; he sent a gift for you." Mom hands me a letter and a small bag.

I sit back and read the letter. *'My love, today I finally get to dedicate myself to you forever, publicly. I'm not sure if you realized yet, but one year ago today is when I knew you were special when I began to fall in love with you. When we met, I was a fraction of the man that I am now. Because of you, I am whole again. You are my heart, my soul, the air that I breathe, my life, my everything. We have created a family and a home together, and today we create a promise of forever. Thank you for allowing me to become your husband and making me the luckiest man alive. Thank you for loving me back, and for giving me the perfect life. I will love you always. Phil.'*

Wiping a few tears from my cheek, I open the bag, finding a small box inside. A note lays on top; 'one diamond for every day I have loved you, one Ruby for every month, and one chain that will circle you, never-ending... like my love.' I pull out the most extravagant bracelet I've ever seen. Everyone in the room gasps at the sight of the white gold, diamond-laden bracelet, with a dozen bright red, heart-shaped rubies. Mom helps me put it on. I can't believe that I'm marrying this man; he means everything to me and treats me like a princess. I give Mom the gift I bought for Phil - a money clip with our monogram. I had it engraved with *'my love, your love, our love, foreve*r'.

As mom leaves, the stylist finishes with my hair. Before long, she brings me over to the mirror; the front looks perfect, swept off my face with loose strands framing my cheeks. She brings a hand-held mirror, allowing me to see the back. It's a masterpiece. She has loose braids twisting to form two small, braided roses, one slightly higher than the other. Nearing the nape of my neck, the hair transforms into a lightly curled pony, off to the side and draping over my shoulder.

"I love it! Who would have thought you could do something like this with hair? Thank you," I gush.

"Oh Miss, we aren't done yet. You still need your veil." The stylist smiles, holding up my floor-length, Italian lace veil. "Now why don't you get your make up

The Climb

done. When you're finished, we'll help you get into your dress and put this beautiful headpiece on you."

∞ ∞ ∞

The next ninety minutes fly by and Dad comes to the room. "Oh my, Trista, you look beautiful. It's time, my dear... the carriage is ready to take us to the vineyard."

Smiling, I take a deep breath in and take my dad's arm as he leads me down the stairs. The entire house is adorned in beautiful white flowers and greenery. My mom, Joanne, and Katie all wait as we take each step. Seeing the approving smiles and tears forming on their lashes, I feel ready for the next step in Phil's and my life together.

The replica Cinderella carriage waits at the front step. The five of us take our seats, and the two large, white horses begin to trot down the rose-petal-covered path to the vineyard. We pull up to a white carpet, and the music starts to play. My two amazing bridesmaids - dressed in flowing, strapless, pale yellow gowns - proceed down the aisle, each carrying one simple calla lily.

Dad helps Mom out of the carriage and then they both help me. My large Cinderella dress makes it fun trying to get in and out of pretty much everything. Before long, the traditional wedding march begins to play and everyone rises. With all eyes on me, I step forward toward the rose-garnished arch, Mom on one side and Dad on the other. Everything's breathtaking, but the best sight of all is at the end of the aisle, staring back at me in astonishment.

With my parents at my side, we begin pacing towards the love of my life - right foot, together, left foot, together. My veil blowing gently in the warm breeze, the large princess skirt and fitted bodice make me feel beautiful. I knew the moment I saw this dress that it was *the one*. Its white satin bodice is covered with beading and rhinestones, with two-inch, off the shoulder sleeves, made from the same Italian lace as my veil. The skirt is a huge ball of tulle and I love it. I'm wearing the necklace and earrings Phil gave me the night he proposed, as well as the bracelet he gave me today. I even have replica glass slippers. For tonight, I really am Cinderella, about to marry Prince Charming. With a small bouquet of calla lilies and red Charlotte roses, I take the next step to join the man I love... the man I will call my husband.

By, Charlotte Blackwell

Chapter 42

Phil

My God... just when I thought Trista couldn't be any more beautiful. As I stand here watching my bride-to-be walk towards me, my heart skips a beat. Tears fill my eyes, knowing that she chose me; after everything we went through to be together, she wants me. I'm the luckiest man alive, and I will never forget it.

As she nears, I step forward, ready to accept her hand from her parents. They meet me at the edge of the altar and place her hand in mine. She's perfect and beautiful and I love her with all my heart. I smile at the woman that completes me, and she smiles back with eyes gleaming, full of hope and love. We both look back to our baby girl sitting in my mom's arms.

"Who gives this woman to this man?" asks the minister.

Mr. Smith speaks up, "Her mother and I do."

"Thank you, you may all be seated," he guides.

Staring at Trista in complete awe, I don't even really know what's going on around me until the minister asks us to exchange vows.

I go first, "Trista, what can I say to express my love to you that I haven't already said? You are the sun, the moon, and the stars to me. You are the love I never thought I'd find and the mother to our daughter. In the last year, you have given me so much more than I ever expected. You and our baby girl are more than I could have ever hoped for, and yet, here you are. Our love happened fast, but it is deep and true. I can't wait to spend the rest of my life with you. One day when we are old and grey, we can sit on the porch, drinking the wine we made here at home and watch our grandchildren play. We can tell them stories of the clumsy girl I literally picked up and carried down a mountain, and how I fell head-over-heels in love with her. You are my everything, and you give me everything. Thank you, my love. I promise to love you for all eternity, with all my heart and soul, no matter what the world throws at us. I will always respect you and cherish every minute we have together. Today I promise to be the best husband you could ask for, and to always know that you are right and I am wrong,"

The guests all chuckle.

"I give you all of me and will strive to give more than my all, for the rest of our lives. I love you, Trista." I finish with a squeeze to her hand.

Trista wipes the tears from her face and begins her vows. "Phil, when we met in Africa, climbing Kilimanjaro, I knew you were an amazing man, but never did I think I would be able to call you *my* amazing man. Everyone knows that I believe your late wife, Sara, brought us together. Because you are so dedicated to those you love, you were there fulfilling her dreams. It couldn't have been sheer luck that we ended up on the same climb; I'm convinced it had to be her. I'm saddened that I can't thank her, but I'm grateful too. Had she not joined the angels, I would not have you or baby Sara to call my own. She will always be my hero, for she gave me life, love, and happiness when she gave me you."

I notice a bright rainbow appear over our vineyard. In this moment, I know it's Sara hearing Trista's thanks and sharing love with us all.

Trista continues, "I still haven't figured out what I did to deserve such a funny, sweet, generous, caring man, but let me tell you, I'm never letting you go. When you came into my life, I finally knew what love was. Even when I thought I'd lost you, I was left with the most amazing memory of our love... our daughter. Luckily, you found us and gave us a reason to live. You give us everything and more. I don't know what I give you in return, but I will give anything and everything I can. It will never be a fraction of the love I have for you. I just don't think there are words or actions that can show you what you mean to me. I do promise to try, every day of my life and more. Thank you for showing me what love truly is, and giving me the opportunity to show it back to you. I love you, Phil," she says, barely able to finish between her tears of joy.

Looking at Trista and listening to her speak renders me unable to hold back my emotions, and tears well up in my eyes. I notice there aren't very many dry eyes around. My late wife's parents are sobbing, Mom and Dad are both tearful, and nearly everyone else is wiping at least a tear or two away. She spoke from the heart - we both did - and I think everyone knows it. Others begin to notice the rainbow, and I can tell they all feel the love behind it; they, too, know it's Sara giving her blessing.

My mom brings baby Sara up to the altar to join us; she looks adorable in the white satin and tulle dress that matches her mommy's. Everyone lets out an 'awe' sound as she smiles, and the minister says, "Phil and Trista have asked to include Sara in the ceremony. Phil, Trista, do you promise to provide for your daughter, to love her with all your hearts and to always be there for her, in good times and bad?"

We both answer, "We do," and smile at our baby girl.

The minister continues, "You have committed yourselves in life and love to Sara and to each other, in front of all these witnesses and God. I welcome you all with God's love. You may present her with your gift."

Pulling out the small box from my inside coat pocket, I open it, and Trista removes the small gold chain with a simple gold heart dangling from it. Together we place the chain around Sara's neck and say, "We promise to always love you and protect you."

With applause from the guests and a little clap from Sara, Mom takes her back to her seat.

Asking for the rings, Mark presents them to the minister, who places them on his bible and says a small prayer.

"Phil, please take the ring for Trista. Do you take Trista to be your wife from this day forward, in sickness and health, for richer or poorer, for life everlasting?"

"I do." Unable to take my eyes off Trista, I slip the band onto her finger.

"Trista, please take the ring for Phil. Do you take Phil to be your husband from this day forward, in sickness and health, for richer or poorer, for life everlasting?"

She smiles and slides the ring onto my finger, while saying, "I do."

"I now pronounce you husband and wife. Phil, you may kiss your bride!" announces the minister.

Grabbing Trista in my arms, I plant the biggest kiss on her and then dip her in my arms. As our guests cheer and clap, I stand her back on her feet. We clasp hands, raising them above our heads and the room erupts in loud applause, as the minister announces, "I now present Mr. and Mrs. Phillip McKay.

Trista grabs Sara in her arms and together, we walk up the aisle as a family.

Chapter 43

Trista

As we walk back up the aisle, I finally take a moment to look around. The vineyard looks magnificent. I didn't notice before, but the guests are all seated on handmade log benches with extravagant carving and woodwork. There's a canopy of greenery and flowers that still allows plenty of sun to shine through, and the white carpeted aisle is adorned on either side with red rose petals. The altar we stood on is also embellished with hand-crafted woodwork. Candle chandeliers hang from stands on either side of the altar, and there is a pleasant scent of vanilla, my favorite. This looks more like a movie star wedding, rather than just some girl from the west coast, but it's so perfect like stolen from a dream.

I don't think I'll ever forget this day; the way Phil looked at me as I walked towards him, the words he said during his vows. I'm so in love with my husband... wow, my *husband*... that's something I would've never expected to say before I met Phil. Together with Sara, we get in the carriage to go have pictures taken. Joanne, Katie, my brother, Marc - who also stood up for Phil - and our parents will join us soon. The guests will be directed to the reception tent for cocktails.

"I can't believe we did it. We pulled off a quickie wedding, Hollywood style," I joke.

"Yeah, we did... but we'll last into eternity, not the sixty days the stars usually do. Thank you again for making me your husband."

"Phil, you don't need to thank me. I should be thanking you for everything you do. What is it that I do to make you love me?"

"Baby, I love you for who you are, everything you do is just an added bonus, and much appreciated." He leans over and presses his lips to mine.

"I love you, too."

By, Charlotte Blackwell

∞ ∞ ∞

Our photos take about an hour. I have a second dress for the reception, so our wedding party takes the baby to mingle with our guests, as Phil and I go to our room, so I can change. Walking into the house, Phil sweeps me off my feet and carries me to our room. How he's managing with my oversized skirt, I don't know.

"Baby, I can't wait till tonight. I need you now," he says while placing me back on my feet.

Our lips meet and move together in unison, as our tongues do a little dance together. He spins me and begins to unlace the corset top of my dress. I feel excitement growing just from his touch. Sliding my dress off, he lifts me out of the skirt, laying me on our bed, my one leg slightly curled around his.

Slow and steady, we make love like never before. I actually *feel* his love, joined as if we are one, moving perfectly in sync. My heart pounds hard with the love I feel for Phil; it takes my breath away to think that he's mine and wants me too. Unable to help myself, I smile, knowing we'll be together forever. A love like ours is too strong and too real to ever let anything come between us. A single tear falls from my eye because this is what true happiness feels like.

∞ ∞ ∞

After only half an hour alone, we redress with lightning speed and make our way to our reception. Standing at the entrance, I straighten my floor-length silk gown. It's perfect for an evening of dancing and fun. The low V-neck is very sensual, and the fitted bodice with tank straps shows every curve. The flowing skirt hangs perfectly over my backside, confirmed by Phil as he taps it and smiles. I feel sexy tonight. I changed my hair to a simple pony - it got a little messed up during our tryst.

Suddenly, I hear my brother over the sound system. "And now I'd like to introduce Phil and Trista McKay, as they share their first dance as husband and wife."

The music starts and Phil leads me to the dance floor, pulling me close for our first dance. The guests surround the dance floor and hold up lit sparklers, swaying to the music. It looks as if a billion stars are all around us. This moment, right here... this is the picture of how I feel when I'm in Phil's arms. I've never been able to describe it, but somehow the wedding planner found a way to show it.

After dinner, while the toasts are going on, Mr. Roberts and his wife, Sara's parents, take the podium for a toast. Her father speaks, "We'd like to make a toast to Trista. You're an amazing woman. You've always accepted our late daughter as part of Phil... as the reason for you two being together. You accepted us as part of Phil's family and never felt threatened by the love he had for her. You honored her by naming your child after her and allowing us to be a third set of grandparents to that beautiful baby girl. Trista, we will never be able to thank you for everything you've done, but we can begin by telling you that we love you like a daughter, and admire you for the love you obviously have for our daughter. Thank you for not letting her memory fade, but instead, embracing it. May you and Phil have an eternity of love, happiness, and good fortune. To Trista," he announces, and raises his glass.

As the clinks of over five hundred glasses ring through the air, I go to the amazing couple at the podium and hug them both. "Thank you for that. I love you both like family as well."

I can't believe how many guests are here. Phil and I must have stood in the receiving line for nearly an hour, everyone wanting to congratulate and hug us. I don't know how many people we haven't had a chance to speak with. Everything's been more than I could've ever asked for. Our five-tier cake is decorated half white, like a wedding dress to represent me, and half black, like a tuxedo to represent Phil. It's pretty cool, I have to say, and each layer is a different flavor.

Tonight's been perfect, but now we are leaving for a two-week honeymoon. Phil won't tell me where he's taking me, but we are leaving Sara here with mom and Joanne. I know they're more than competent... I'm just not sure if I'm ready to not see her smiling face for that long. I'm going to miss her like mad, but I must admit, it will be nice to get away alone with Phil. I'm sure wherever we go, it'll be an adventure.

By, Charlotte Blackwell

Chapter 44

Phil

To keep our honeymoon a surprise from Trista, I booked us a private jet. The staff is under strict orders not to spill the beans. I can't wait to see her face. I know this is one of the places on her bucket list, so I jumped at the chance to take her. I want to show her the world.

"Come on, Phil, will you tell me where we're going already? We're over thirty thousand feet in the air. I have no escape," she begs.

"You really don't do well with surprises, do you?" I chuckle.

"No, I was the girl who used to unwrap Christmas gifts beforehand and rewrap them again. I get so excited I just can't wait. Please, tell me."

"Nope, not getting a thing outta me, chickie."

"Fine then, but maybe I should make a little confession to you… something I've been scared to tell you because I don't want you to think any differently of me."

"Baby, nothing you could say could ever make me love you less."

"Well, I know it bothers you when I'm hard on myself."

"Yeah, it really does."

"There's a reason for that. See… I had a boyfriend before who used to tell me that I was useless, ugly and stupid. Complete emotional abuse that hurt me to the core. It's been very difficult for me to think differently of myself. Obviously, I didn't stay with him very long, but my boss at the bank used to make me feel the same way. I guess after hearing that for so long, I just started to believe it, and it's been difficult for me to understand why you don't think the same."

"Oh Trista, they're both idiots. You never deserved to be treated like that. If anyone ever does that to you again, I'll beat the shit out of them. You're perfect."

"But… I don't really have anything to offer you. I'm not as intelligent as you; my life has no real direction…"

The Climb

"You're perfect, end of story." In an attempt to quiet her, I move closer on the plush sofa the plane is equipped with and kiss her. With a slight push of my body into hers, she lays back. This woman, my wife does something to me; I can't keep my hands off her, I can't keep my mind off her. I wish we could just spend the first year of our marriage in bed, making love the entire time. She's so goddamned sexy, I let out a slight growl as I nuzzle her neck. It doesn't take long before our clothes are strewn all over the cabin of the plane, and silently, I hope the staff doesn't come in to check on us... they might get a good show.

Trista pulls me close to her, skin to skin, and runs both hands up the sides of my face, weaving her fingers in my hair as our lips lock. Things get slightly more intense than we ever have before, maybe the thrill of being caught, or the thrill of joining the mile-high club. I'm not sure what it is, but it's always amazing with her.

"Love you, baby... that was amazing," I huff.

"Love you, too. Thank you, times five," she chuckles.

∞ ∞ ∞

Once composed and dressed, we take our seats back on the sofa, hands wrapped tight together. I push the call button for the flight attendant.

"Yes sir, how may I help you?" she asks.

"May we please have some champagne and fresh fruit?" I request.

"Actually, I'd love water as well, please," Trista requests.

"Of course, I'll just be a minute." The flight attendant takes her leave.

She comes back within moments, hands Trista her water, and places two champagne flutes filled with sparkling bubbly and an assorted fruit tray on the table. Trista and I enjoy our snack, and I sip on the champagne while Trista drinks her water. I guess I worked her well enough to dehydrate her.

After a thirteen-hour flight, we're ready to land. Trista looks at me and asks again, "Can you tell me *now* where we are?"

"Welcome to Peru, baby. We're going to climb the Inca Trail," I say, with a smile.

"ARE YOU KIDDING ME?" she screams. "You brought me to Machu Picchu? This has always been a dream of mine. Thank you so much, Phil."

"You're welcome. I remembered you mentioned it as a bucket list trip. I want all your dreams to come true."

"Phil, all my dreams *did* come true… the moment I met you." She kisses me. "Well, maybe I can give you a little surprise for our honeymoon as well."

"You don't have to. Having you as my wife is all I need."

"Maybe, but I hope you like it. It's pretty big, and takes months of preparation," she giggles.

"Okay, now you have piqued my interest," I admit with curiosity.

Chapter 45

Trista

ith a smile, I look deep into Phil's eyes and say, "Sara is going to be a big sister... I'm pregnant."

By, Charlotte Blackwell

The End

Made in the USA
San Bernardino, CA
25 October 2018